First Kiss One

CHRISTMAS TO EASTER

FOUR 45 MINUTE READS

First Kiss One

CHRISTMAS TO EASTER

FOUR 45 MINUTE READS

LEE WILLIAMSON

Contents

Story One: Christmas Kiss

The Pub

The air from the cooler wafts over my face, a welcome relief from the alcohol laden fug in the bar. It is busy tonight. Busier than a regular Friday.

'Get used to it,' Stan, the bar owner says, 'It'll be like this up until Christmas. Everyone and their dog'll be here ordering up their Christmas cheer.'

Plonking the wine into an ice filled bucket, I take it down the other end of the bar to the group of friends standing in a relatively quiet corner.

'Thanks, Chris, you're a star,' blonde haired Lucie tells me, handing over her card.

I flash her a smile and take it, tapping the charge before handing it back.

'It's busy tonight,' her boyfriend Dave attempts to strike up a conversation, I can just hear him over the noise.

Any other night I would have stopped and chatted with the group of friends I met on my first shift five months ago. I've gotten to know them pretty well. I catch a glimpse of Leena's red hair and my heart does a flip. I hate to miss an opportunity to talk to her.

'Yep,' I say, glancing down the bar, which is now about four deep. A couple of those squashed up front direct daggers my way. 'Gotta go,' I say, reluctantly turning back to the waiting horde.

'Come see us on your break,' Tony yells over the din. 'We'll shout you a drink. You'll need it by then.' The blue-eyed tech genius winks.

'Over here,' a voice shouts, and that's it, I'm rushed off my feet, literally.

The bar I tended in uni was nothing like this swanky, Central London watering hole full of traders and tech-preneurs who think the world revolves around them. I miss the few locals who haunted the pub back home.

I don't get my first break until after ten. Once Stan relieves me, I push my way through the bar towards Tony, hoping for a chance to talk tech, and maybe exchange a few words with the lovely Leena.

'Mate, you look exhausted. Here, have some bubbles,' Tony greets me, pushing a glass of sparkling liquid my way.

I would have preferred a beer, but with what I get paid and the cost of living in London, I can't afford to be choosy.

'Thanks,' I say, taking the glass and downing half in one go. As the bubbles evaporate on my tongue there's a sharp tug on my taste buds, and moments later the alcohol rushes to my head.

'So what's happening tonight?' I ask.

'Well, I got a promotion.' he points to the wine bottle. 'Hence the bubbles.'

'Congratulations, mate,' I say, clapping him on the shoulder.

He shrugs it off, almost embarrassed by the attention. 'Lucie's trying to organise us for New Year's, and Leena's bemoaning Christmas.'

At the mention of her name, Leena towards us. 'I'm not whingeing about Christmas, just work Christmas parties.'

Under her gaze my heart pounds, and my palms sweat. My tongue swells to twice the size and I lose the power of speech. I'm forced to watch as Tony, who's known the goddess Leena forever and is completely unaffected by her beauty, responds.

'How does it go again? Why does it have to be on a weekend? Why do we have to take partners? Why is it so formal?' He teases. 'I don't understand why you don't pass and spend the night with us.'

Leena punches Tony on the arm, and it's not a lite tap either. 'Yep, great idea, bozo. Not all of us are geniuses. Some of us have to schmooze the bosses to rise through the ranks.'

She runs a hand through her thick, long hair, sweeping it off her face. 'And it isn't my fault all the men in my life with are hooked up with my best friends.' She flashes a grin at the girls, taking the sting from her words.

Antonio holds up his hands. 'Hey, I don't have a girl-friend and you didn't ask me.'

Leena drapes an arm over his shoulder. 'And any other night I would take you along. Unfortunately, Robert's told me about his plans for the weekend, and I won't spoil that.'

Antonio leans down and kisses the top of Leena's head. 'Yep, I'd have to do some quick talking if I ruined his surprise.'

'What about Chris?' Cecily says. 'He's not dating anyone?' She turns sparkling blue eyes on me, an eyebrow raised in query.

'Um…ah…no.' *Smooth bro, way to sweep a girl off her feet.*

I stare at the ground, trying to compose myself. I've a shift tomorrow night, that's as good an excuse as any to get out of this awkward situation. When I look up, Leena is standing in front of me, cat green eyes level with mine, her face mock beseeching.

'Would you, Chris? I promise it won't be too much of a chore. It's at a swanky place with great food and free drinks. And, who knows, you might meet someone you like.'

'Go on, Chris,' Cecily adds. 'Some of her workmates are real pillocks—it's all that startup venture capital bullshit. But there are also some cool people, and a few are techies so you might make some contacts.' She slips her arm through Tony's and leans her head on his shoulder.

With the three of them staring at me, I want to say no, but the word is stuck in my throat.

Ever since I met Leena all I've wanted to do is to ask her out, but I've never plucked up the courage. She is so confident, and beautiful, and… amazing—way out of my league.

Don't get me wrong, I do all right. Years of surfing have given me a decent body, which I keep toned in the local pool, and a tan that hasn't faded much yet. When I look in the mirror, I'm not horrified. I might not be Chris Hemsworth, but I'm a solid Liam.

Still, if I could pluck up the courage to ask her out, this is not what I would plan for a first date—a work Christmas party with everyone getting drunk, trying too hard to enjoy themselves, and crying in their drinks at the end of the evening.

'All right,' I say. 'I'll go. Text me the details.'

I thread my way back through the crowded bar to finish my shift, my stomach churning in a mixture of disappointment and anticipation.

Party Night

I hunch into my borrowed coat as the damp permeates my bones in the way only London weather can. It's supposed to snow tonight. The English always hope it'll snow for Christmas. It's such a big deal they even bet on it happening.

As I turn into the East End street Leena texted me to pick her up from, I wonder how my family and friends are doing. A wave of sadness hits me. I pull out my phone and text my brother.

Happy almost Christmas.

It's early morning in Sydney so I don't expect a response. I'll call tomorrow.

My phone buzzes. *Dude, it's 5am.*

I chuckle. *The barbie needs cleaning or there'll be no prawns for Chrissie lunch.*

This time the response is immediate. *Car's packed. We're heading up the coast in an hour. Christmas at the beach.*

Call you later, I end, wishing I was there. Perhaps next year I'll be working in my dream job and I'll head home for a proper Christmas in the sun.

Ah, number 53, I've arrived. The building's one of many redeveloped warehouses lining the street. Before pressing the button, I try to shake off my melancholy.

So, I'm not at home, and this is not the first date I imagined with Leena. But, it *is* a date—anything could happen. A car pulls up behind me and honks as I press the buzzer.

'Chris?' A female voice asks over the intercom.

'Yep.'

'Is that the taxi too?'

I turn to find a traditional London black cab idling by the curb. Cool. I can normally only afford the underground, so this'll be something to tick off the bucket list.

'Yep.'

'I'll be done in a mo.'

Sheltering in the doorway out of the drizzle, I angle myself so I can see through the slat of safety glass. It's uncomfortable compared to waiting in the cab, but I'm rewarded by a glimpse of Leena as she steps out of the lift.

She's wearing an off the shoulder sparkling emerald cocktail dress that clings to her curves in all the right places. By the time she joins, me the dress is a slip of green hidden under a black coat she is doing up around the creamy skin of her neck.

For a moment I wonder what it would be like to move the stray strands of hair out of the way and brush my lips across the skin peeking out from her collar. The moment is gone when she scolds me with a curt, 'Chris, you should have waited in the cab.'

I chuckle as I open the car door for her, and attempt to lighten the mood. 'What, and have my mother's voice in my head all evening berating me for my lack of manners?'

Before she says anything to make things more awkward, I push the door shut and duck around the cab. I plonk into the seat on the other side, struggling to arrange my coat.

'Where to love?' A west Indian accent drifts from the front. The cabbie's already identified who is running this show.

'The Hilton, Hyde Park, thanks,' Leena says, settling back as the cabbie closes the window and slides away from the curb.

'Thank you for doing this for me.' Leena speaks to me, but stares out the window. 'I hope it wasn't too much trouble sorting a black-tie outfit on such short notice.'

I don't want to tell her that the only thing I'm wearing that I owned before this morning are my underwear and my shoes. Fortunately, Tony put me onto a great op-shop selling second-hand tuxes and dress shirts.

'They're last seasons or older, but they're cheaper than renting,' he'd told me.

They *were* cheap and they had my size. While my suit and shirt spent some time in a two-hour dry cleaners, I nipped round to Tony's to pick up a tie and coat. I'll be living on baked beans for the next month, but it'll be worth it—I hope.

'No worries, I always travel with a suit,' I joke, and she manages a weak smile.

The conversation falters. *Well, this is fun.* I mentally shake myself. If this was any other night, or any other girl, I'd be chatting away trying to make a connection.

'So, anything I need to know before we enter the lion's den?'

She pulls her gaze away from the passing scenery. 'Sorry, Chris. I hate these things. I shouldn't have dragged you into my nightmare.'

Her fingers twist in her lap. She's as nervous as I am—perhaps for a different reason, but at least it's something we have in common. I smile, hoping to put her at ease.

'I assure you, I'm perfectly house trained, and can even hold a half decent conversation. I won't show you up.'

My attempt at a joke falls flat. A stricken look crosses her face. 'I didn't mean...'

'Leena, calm down. We're going to eat a meal and a few with your workmates, and when you've put in a solid appearance we can leave. No one will be bored. No one will be embarrassed. And, if we're lucky, we might have fun.'

Her shoulders relax and she returns my smile. 'You're awfully sure of yourself given you haven't met my work-mates yet.'

Good, this is the Leena I know—sassy and confident.

'After working in a bar in London, I think I can handle anything they throw at me,' I tell her.

A frown creases her brow. 'Ah, about that…'

She doesn't need to say it. Not everyone is comfortable dating a bartender.

'It's ok. You can tell them I'm here working on a pitch to Pinewood.' I reassure her. 'I won't be offended.'

Her smile returns. 'You know, I forgot about your other job.'

I laugh. 'Hardly a job yet. My interview isn't until after Christmas.'

She takes my hand in hers and I almost don't hear her words my heart is beating so fast. 'Chris, don't talk like that, even if you are joking. To get ahead in life you need to believe you will succeed.'

'We're here, love,' the cabbie calls, and our brief moment of connection is gone.

Fish Out of Water

The tiramisu melts in my mouth and I stifle a groan.

"It's good, isn't it,' Anabeth, the girl on my left says, her chocolate brown eyes twinkling.

'Good doesn't describe it,' I tell her, rolling my eyes.

She laughs and takes another spoonful.

I turn to Leena, but she's still talking to the head of finance sitting on her other side. Anabeth's dinner companion is chatting to the waitress, or more specifically—chatting her up.

'He's a terrible flirt,' she tells me.

'Don't you mind him flirting with other women?'

She grins. 'Hell no. He's my brother, and I wish one of them would stick around long enough to take him off my hands.'

Her brother half-turns, throws her a dirty look, then follows the waitress out of the dining room.

Leena touches my arm and I turn to find her standing beside the man she has spent most of the evening speaking to. 'Neville and I are headed to the bar to discuss an idea I've had,' she tells me. 'Do you want to join us?'

My eyes drift to my half-eaten dessert, then back to her. 'Perhaps when I'm finished,' I say, but she's already following her boss out.

I finish the tiramisu, and Leena's untouched one, and finish my coffee. Anabeth excuses herself to go find her brother and I head to the bar. Leena is surrounded by a gaggle of men preening and vying for her attention. I see I'm not needed and I head to the bar to order a whiskey.

'Gin and tonic,' a voice beside me says, and I move to allow Anabeth in beside me.

She was bright and bubbly company over dinner, and I hope maybe she will stay for a bit and keep me company.

'Lost your brother again?'

She laughs, 'Yes, but he'll be back. It's all about the chase for him.'

In her heels she is almost as tall as I am. As she waits for her drink, I allow myself to appreciate her willowy form, showcased in a violet ankle-length lace number.

'I see Leena's still talking shop,' she says, turning to me.

We turn as one towards her group. Leena appears unaware of the hold she has over them as she debates the merits of investing in additional functionality for the app, and they follow her every word.

'Yep,' I say, unable to drag my gaze away.

'You've got it bad, huh?'

I force myself to turn away and pick up my drink.

'Sorry, what was that?'

She stares at me over the rim of her glass. 'You've got the Leena bug. It's okay. Most of the guys at work have it. We girls'd all hate her if she wasn't so unaware of the affect she has on them.'

I'm uncomfortable spilling my heart to a total stranger, especially one as attractive as Anabeth.

'I'm just her plus one for a night out at a swanky restaurant.'

'Sure.' She quickly hides a brief flash of sympathy as she places her hand on my arm. 'If you say so.'

The sudden rush of heat from my neck to my face has me hoping I'm not actually blushing. Desperately to change the subject, I ask, 'Do you work in finance too?'

She tucks a strand of purple streaked silver hair behind an ear, revealing a dragon ear clip that brings a smile to my lips. She is so not what I expected from a workmate of Leena's.

'No, nothing that exciting. I'm a coding a new module for the app.'

Anabeth's brother choses that moment to join us.

'So the waitress blew you off,'she teases him.

He ignores her. 'Don't listen to her, Chris. She and her mates designed the app at uni, and she's the only one they kept on after the buy-out.'

I assess my companion with fresh eyes. She is intent on squishing the lime in her drink with the straw. Her brother's comment has obviously made her uncomfortable, and I feel a protective urge to put her at ease.

'Really? You're millionaire coder?' I joke.

'I wish.' She smiles shyly. 'The buyout was small and I opted for shares in the company anyway. I won't see a dime beyond my salary until we start making a profit.'

'Smart move,' I tell her. 'From what Leena says, it's going to be the new Twitter.'

Her cheeks redden, and she seems to be finding her drink fascinating. I frantically think of something else to say to make this fey girl smile, but I'm distracted by a presence at my side.

'I see you're keeping yourself entertained, Chris,' Leena purrs and my heart flips.

'Yep. Anabeth and… um Robbie here are filling me in on the background to the app.' Pleased I managed to string a coherent sentence together, I grin like an idiot.

'Would you like to come and meet some of the board?' she asks, linking her arm through mine.

With her body this close, it's difficult to think of anything other than what it might be like to pull her into my arms and kiss those cherry red lips. Unfortunately, her lure will not overcome my aversion to the men she's with. A few months working in the pub has taught me I will never have anything in common with them.

'Thanks,' I tell her, 'I'm fine here.'

A frown creases her perfect brow, and she glances side-long at Anabeth. 'If you're sure I can't tempt you away…' she pauses, giving me the chance to change my mind. When she realises I'm not moving, she says, 'All right then.'

I watch her body sway the sparkling green sheath as she returns to her group of admirers.

'Interesting,' Robbie says, bringing my attention back to the bar.

I take a gulp of whiskey before asking, 'What is?'

'The ice queen seems to have a soft spot for you.' He playfully punches me on the arm.

I turn slightly so I can't be tempted to look her way. 'She was just being polite. Making sure I'm okay.'

'Sure,' Robbie says and slides onto a stool.

In another room music starts up and a few people leave the bar. Anabeth and Robbie stay, and I notice Leena's group does too.

'So, Chris, what are you doing in London? Taking a year out and working as a waiter?' Anabeth is the first person tonight to ask me anything about myself.

I laugh. 'Not a waiter, I work in a bar.'

'Hopefully somewhere nice, away from all these London wankers... oops that was rude.' She takes a gulp of her drink in an attempt to hide her embarrassment.

I raise my eyebrows in mock surprise. 'You don't like your workmates?'

She shrugs. 'Not many of them, no.'

'Well I'm not too keen on them either. I serve them—or people like them—and we have nothing in common.'

'So why do you work there?' Robbie asks.

'One of mum's old friends owns the bar. He's let me have the room above for free. I couldn't have afforded to come over and spend time in London otherwise.'

Anabeth nods. Everyone who lives in London shares my pain. 'Are you saving to do Europe?'

I shake my head. 'That wasn't the plan.'

Suddenly I'm shy about telling her why I'm in England. Everyone else glazes over and changes the subject when

I talk about movies and animation. Only Tony has taken me seriously—helping me on my portfolio, and to hone my presentation.

Anabeth tilts her head to the side and studies me for a moment. Perhaps sensing my discomfort, she says, 'Sorry, I ask a lot of questions. You don't have to answer.'

'No, it's ok.' Suddenly I have the urge tell her about my job interview. 'Since uni I've been working for a movie production company. I gave up my job to come over here to interview for the Pinewood special effects team. In my spare time brushing up my presentation and portfolio.'

Anabeth's eyes light up and she leans in. 'Cool. What sort of special effects do you do?'

'Mostly digital, but I've done some stop frame animation on short films,' I tell her.

'Anything I might know?'

'Ana's a movie buff,' Robbie adds, before sliding off the stool. 'If you guys are going to film talk, I'm going to dance.' He saunters away in time to the music, scanning the crowd for a potential partner.

'The short films were only released in Australia,' I tell Anabeth.

'What about the other movies you worked on?'

'There's an action one that should be coming out early next year,' I admit.

She frowns, 'Action's not really my thing…'

'Mine neither, but you take the work where you can get it.'

Anabeth chews her bottom lip, then blurts out, 'Don't I know it. I'm kinda not enjoying working for the startup as much as I thought I would. I think I'll wait around for the next launch, and then I'm off.'

'Will you do something yourself, or join another company?'

'I'm not sure. I want to develop something that makes people's lives better. Our app was supposed to do that, now they just want it to make more money. So… I'm thinking maybe freelance for a while.'

I slip onto the bar stool Robbie vacated and order another drink. It's so refreshing talking someone who understands about giving up work that isn't particularly satisfying.

'I'm hoping if I get into Pinewood I'll get a bit more variety, and a bit more control over what I get to do,' I tell her, and she nods in understanding.

The next hour flies by as I start to enjoy myself for the first time tonight.

Eavesdroppers Never Hear Good

Out of the corner of my eye I catch Leena heading for the cloakrooms. Wondering if she's thinking of leaving, I excuse myself and follow her towards the back lobby. I catch a glimpse of green as the door to the ladies' room closes.

Finding I need the men's room, I head there, thinking I'll catch Leena on the way back. I finish up and am washing my hands when I hear disembodied female voices.

One of them is definitely Leena. I step back. Yep, her voice is clear if I stand here. I nip into the cubical and close the door.

Do I feel guilty? Hell no. What person doesn't want to find out what's being said about them by a girl they're interested in?

'—doesn't see me as anything other than Tony's friend.'

If that's me she's talking about, then she couldn't be more wrong.

'Why don't you let him know you fancy him. Anabeth certainly is,' an unknown voice answers.

She is? A smile curves my lips as I think of Anabeth leaning towards me, eagerly arguing why I should give Doctor Who a second chance. Or how she tucks her hair behind her ear when she's making a point—like telling me books are always better than movies—the eyes of her dragon ear clip flashing in agreement.

'I'm not so sure.' Leena's voice interrupts my reverie. 'I don't want to lead him on. I mean, I'm not looking to make it into anything, I only want someone for tonight.'

I'm good with that, I mentally send to her. One night can turn into two, or maybe more.

'You're a modern woman. You can do this.'

Yes you can! I cheer her on.

'I don't know…'

'If you were a man, we wouldn't be having this conversation. He'd do it without all this soul searching.'

Woah, hold on there. Not all men. Besides, *I* would be using tonight to convince Leena we could have so much more.

Would you though? The devil on my other shoulder weighs in. *So far she hasn't shown any interest in you, and she just called you Tony's friend, not* my *friend.*

Shh, I tell it. *I'm listening.* But I'm too late. The only noise coming from next door is the echo of a door closing.

I let myself out of the cubicle and head back to the bar, hopeful tonight will end exactly as I'd hoped. I can see Leena's dress through the door. In a couple of strides I'm beside her.

'Are you ready to go?' I ask, hoping after the conversation I overheard she'll say yes.

She doesn't answer, but carries on searching the room. Was I wrong? Was she talking about someone else? The group she was with had found a bank of chairs, and they're waving her over. She holds up a finger, then turns to me.

'I want to leave,' she tells me. Her eye-slide towards the group suggests otherwise.' But I'll never have another opportunity like this to put my ideas to the board members. You understand, don't you?'

She reaches up and runs her fingers along the lapel of my suit, and my eyes focus on her hand. I do understand, and I would do the same if it were my career. I open my mouth to tell her just that, but don't get a chance. She grabs my tie and tugs me into a darkened corner, before pulling my head towards hers.

Her lips are firm on mine, taint of whiskey and something sweet. My mouth is moving against hers and I can't think of anything else but her lips on mine and the warmth spreading from my belly. She nips at my lower lip and I snake an arm around her back, intending to pull her against me. She steps back before I can tighten my grip.

'Later,' she says, her eyes sparkling as she sashays away.

My eyes follow her, but not with longing. Leena is an accomplished, sexy woman, and her kiss promising more later was more than I could have expected from tonight. I should be elated, but instead I feel…empty.

I drag my gaze away, confused, to lock eyes with Anabeth across the room. The hurt I find there adds to the rush of emotion. She draws her bottom lip between her teeth, shakes her head, then turns on her heel. In moments she disappears towards the coat check.

My body is frozen in place. I half turn towards Leena, thinking I'd join her. No, they don't want me with them, any more than I want their company. I return my attention to Anabeth in time to see her enter the lift.

The only reason I've enjoyed this evening is leaving and still I can't force my body to move. At the very least I should apologise to her. But for what? *Leena* kissed *me*. And why does that matter to Anabeth? It's not like we had anything going? Or did we?

Then it hits me like a punch to the stomach and my legs start moving of their own accord. Weaving through the tables I find the universe is against me, slowing me down as people move chairs or themselves into my path, forcing me to dodge obstacles.

Finally, I'm out. The coat check takes an age to find my coat. I haul it on as I rush down the stairs hoping to catch Anabeth's lift in the lobby. I'm too late.

Zigzagging through a surprisingly busy entranceway, I push the heavy glass doors and search the street for her. There she is, a couple of blocks away, walking, heading back into Central London.

Trafalgar Square

'Anabeth.' My voice is muffled by the drone of traffic. Doesn't this city ever sleep?

I glance warily up at the cloud laden sky. The incessant London drizzle has stopped, but the ground is still slippery underfoot as I take off at a brisk walk after her.

Anabeth is fast, even in heels. I almost catch her up around Archway, but the lights change before I can get there. I call again. Why is she ignoring me? I fall into pace with her around Green Park.

'Anabeth,' I say, tapping her on the shoulder.

She starts, half turns towards me with a can of something in her hand, then relaxes. Placing the container back in her bag, she reaches up and takes out her ear pods.

I shake my head. 'Are you mad? You shouldn't be walking alone at night round here, let alone with ear pods in.'

Her hand sweeps out, gesturing to the passing cars. 'I'm not alone. Besides I've done karate for years. And if that doesn't work, I always have pepper spray handy.'

'Still, a woman alone…'

'A woman should be able to walk alone wherever and whenever she wants, just as a man does. I refuse to be limited by my gender.'

She glares at me all purple under the street lights, and fierce as. I can't help it, I smile at her. This is not how I thought this would go. Then again, I'm not sure what I expected when I ran out after her. Now I'm standing there, all goofy and tongue-tied and unsure what to do next.

'Ah… at least let me walk you home,' I say, feeling seventeen and taking Kylie Simons to our Year 12 Formal awkward—all arms and legs, and commonsense gone.

'Why?'

The single word is like a slap to my senses. Why should she let me walk her home? Why do I want to walk her home? Why am I here? Or all of the above?

'Because it's the right thing to do,' I tell her, and it sounds weak to my own ears— more so after her speech on female independence.

She blows out a breath and the anger drains from her body. 'Chris, go back to Leena. You clearly have something more going on there than you let on.'

Leena? In my rush to catch Anabeth I'd forgotten about her. I should let her know where I am. Or, will she even notice I'm gone until she's ready for her booty call?

Anabeth, taking my moment of confusion as a sign we're done, turns on her heel and carries on walking. I fall into step beside her. We continue alongside Green Park for a while. Anabeth doesn't put her ear buds back in, which I take as a good sign.

As we turn onto St. James Street we still haven't spoken, and the silence is like a weight between us. I have to say something, but everything running through my head at the moment is perhaps not best discussed with the woman walking beside me—well not if I want to make a good impression that is.

There is no way I can explain that for months I have fantasised about dating Leena, about holding her in my arms and getting to know every luscious inch of her body. And less than half an hour ago I had her right where I wanted her. Yep, that would really go down well.

Now I'm here because Anabeth left, and my world quaked. All I could think of as I walked to catch her up was, what if I never saw her again? I'd never know whether she thought the new Taika Waititi film was funny or not? And I promised to show her why Vegemite on toast is so great.

Silly things to be thinking of, and not things I can say out loud now to break this uncomfortable silence. How can I tell her I couldn't let all those little things we spoke about, of those possibilities of future conversations, disappear for a kiss, or a one-night stand.

So, I don't say any of that. Instead, I ask, 'Do you live close?'

A half-smile appears at the edge of her lips, showing off a dimple. 'Worried you won't be able to find your way back?' she asks.

I pull out my phone. 'Google Maps,' I say. 'Just wondering how far a crazy English woman is prepared to walk alone at night, in high heels when it's threatening to snow.'

That brings on a full-on chuckle. 'We Brits always hope it will snow around Christmas. And it always threatens, but never does.'

'So?'

'I live in a flat over a bookshop on Charing Cross Road. Not too much further.'

I raise an eyebrow. 'Man, that must cost a bit to rent.'

'Are all you Aussies so blunt?' she asks.

Her tone is humorous, so I know I haven't offended her. 'Probably,' I say.

'I work Saturdays for my uncle in the shop, and in return he doesn't charge me too much for the flat. It suits me because it's walking distance to work, and I love books.'

'Nice,' I say.

Now the lull in the conversation feels normal. All too soon we arrive at the National Gallery and turn the corner, entering Trafalgar Square. My breath catches, and when Anabeth stops walking I realise I must have sighed out loud.

Trafalgar Square is pretty iconic at the best of times, and I often have to pinch myself when I walk around it to make sure I'm really here. At night time, under the glow of lights, with a dark, cloudy sky as a backdrop, it's breath taking.

Something cold touches my nose, and I'm about to curse the London rain when the world becomes a vision of glitter and ice as snow begins to fall. My mouth stretches into the widest grin and I allow Anabeth to haul me into the square.

I stretch my arms out and spin around like a child, giddy with the joy of it. When I stop, Anabeth is watching me, her eyes bright with laughter, enjoying my happiness.

At that moment the world fades, there is only Anabeth and me. I step towards her. A flash of fear crosses her face and I pause.

'Why are you here, Chris?'

'For this,' I say as I pull her closer.

My eyes lock with hers and I lower my head, brushing her lips gently with mine. When she doesn't pull away, I close my eyes and deepen the kiss. Wrapping my arms around her, her warmth presses against me, and I shudder as her fingers reach up and tangle themselves in my hair.

Her body moulds to mine as if it has always meant to be there, and intense heat melts my limbs. My last coherent thought is, 'Yes, I'm here for this.'

Story Two: A New Years Kiss

Late Again

I thread my way through the crowded streets, rushing against the flow of people. My stiff fingers struggle to obey as I try to fit my earrings through the holes in my lobes without losing my phone. Everyone else is heading to the harbour for a view of the fireworks as I hurry through the cobbled streets of Sydney's Rocks to join my friends.

When I'd organised to meet everyone at Antonio's for midnight, I'd had no idea my shift in the Accident and Emergency Department wouldn't end until an hour before midnight.

My phone pings, it's Kelli: *Margarita waiting for you. Get here already.* I don't have time to answer if I want to be there before the fireworks signal in the new year.

I risk a quick glance at my phone screen—11:50. The band will be playing their last couple of songs. The wait staff will be rushing between the tables making sure everyone has a drink for midnight. My friends will be right up the front, dancing in a group, hyped to be together to farewell the old year.

Ouch! My heel catches in a crack in the pavement, and wrenches slightly. I give it a tentative wriggle. Whew, it's just a twinge. I need to pay attention to where I'm going. Not far now, and I don't want to fall at the last hurdle.

I'm moving faster as the number of people in the back streets dwindles. Music from the concert playing under the Harbour Bridge is an eerie backdrop to the click clack of my heels hitting the cobble stones.

Almost there. I round the corner and can see the bouncer standing outside the restaurant entrance about halfway down the street. He's talking to a group of people. I speed up as the three couples stalk off angrily in the opposite direction and he shrugs his shoulders. My stomach churns. This isn't looking good.

Ping! My phone again. I can't risk checking Kelli's message. I run the last couple of steps to Antonio's, no mean feat in these heels. Another couple are in front of me, and the bouncer is turning them away. 'Sorry, it's packed inside, I can't let anyone in until someone comes out.'

Their heads hang and they push past me to try another option back along the street.

'Hi Tony,' I say in greeting, confident my friends will have sorted my late entry with our favourite restaurant's regular doorman.

My phone pings, and Kelli's message flashes: *Too late, they've shut the doors.* I glance up into Tony's sad brown eyes. 'Sorry, darl, I'm under strict orders—it's strictly one in one out.'

I almost drop to the pavement there and then. The only thing stopping me is that my retro orange tone shift dress is new. My mind goes blank as I stare at the plate glass window framing the revellers inside.

What now? Back down to the harbour to see the New Year in with strangers? My weary body tells me it's not worth it. Without my friends to celebrate it's just another night. My exhausted mind agrees. After a twelve-hour shift today, home is sounding mighty good.

I turn to head there. My phone pings and I glance down, *Sorry :-(.*

'Ten,' the crowd inside calls.

My heel catches between two cobbles and, as I attempt to right myself, my phone falls to the ground. I would have followed if not for two strong arms wrapping around me, setting me back on my feet.

'Nine.'

'Thank you,' I say, expecting Tony to let me go.

'Eight.'

Instead I find myself pec height, facing a Pink Floyd retro t-shirt—and a well-muscled chest it is too, I acknowledge as my fingers spread across its firm planes. At the same time, it works out this is not Tony.

'Seven.'

'Are you okay?' A deep voice asks. I raise my eyes and find myself captured by startling cornflower blue eyes rimmed with lashes most girls would die for.

'Six.'

My heart is pounding, and my limbs tingle as a slow warmth spreads from my belly as it leans in to firm male flesh. I nod, unable to pull a coherent sentence together.

'Five.'

His mouth breaks into a lazy smile. My heart flutters, and my eyes widen with surprise at the desire coursing through me. *Come on, it hasn't been that long since Ben and I broke up.*

'Four.'

An arm releases me and my rescuer reaches to tuck long wavy brown hair behind his ear. My eyes follow the muscled forearm, before taking a step away. I need some distance to get my head straight.

'Three.'

His grin widens as if he knows the affect he is having on me. My heel catches again and the arm around my waist tightens, before steadying me back towards the footpath.

'Two.'

'I think you should stick to the path,' he purrs as he hands me my phone.

'Thank you,' I say, proud my power of speech has recovered.

'One.'

'Oh, the pleasure is all mine,' he says, his eyes darkening, and I see my rising desire reflected there.

Thwiff. The sky lights up with the first of the fireworks.

'Happy New Year.'

His head lowers and as his lips touch mine my body explodes. I reach up, locking my fingers behind his neck and pull him closer, my lips greedily tasting him. My fingers entwine in the long locks of his hair as his arms pull me to him until my body is melded to his.

His tongue parts my lips and teases the inside of my mouth, sending shivers down my spine. His hands run down my back and every nerve in my body is attuned to him. I am on the brink of an abyss. Time stops and all there is his him and I, and the fireworks we're making and I lose myself to the moment.

'Harry. HARRY!'

The insistent call comes from close by, and my lips are slowly released.

'Busy here, mate.' His breath caresses my cheek as he speaks.

'Breaks over.'

Regret slides across his face. He nuzzles into my neck and I moan softly. Raising his head, he softly kisses may lips once more.

'I'll be finished in an hour. Meet me inside?' he whispers.

I nod, unable to speak.

His lips brush lightly against mine, then my knight in shining armour jogs down the alleyway and disappears round the back of the restaurant.

Before my body has cooled from his touch an arm slips through mine. 'Since you couldn't get in, we thought we'd join you out here. Let's go party at the harbour,' Kelli says.

In moments I am surrounded by my group of laughing, tipsy friends, who drag me back the way I have come. I glance over my shoulder, half-thinking to go back, before I allow myself to be carried away by the flow.

New Year's Day

'Why didn't you say you wanted to go back to the restaurant, Hannah?' Kelli throws a cushion and I duck.

'Because New Year is for friends,' I shoot back.

'Nah, New Year's totally for romance and kissing random strangers.' She puckers up and blows me a kiss.

Everyone should have a friend like Kelli—fun, irreverent, and always on my side. I release a sigh. She can also see right through me, which can sometimes be irritating.

'Because it seemed… juvenile… or desperate to change my plans because of one kiss.' My fingers pluck at the cover of the cushion resting on my lap.

Kelli leans in. 'But it was a pretty amazing kiss, right?'

I nod, my lips burning with the memory.

'Right, it's settled. We're going to track this guy down.'

She uncurls her legs, stands and heads for her bedroom. Stopping at her door, she half turns and asks, 'Are you coming?'

I frown. 'Coming where?'

'Antonio's. He'll be open for lunch. You and I should go and ask him who the mysterious guy in the Pink Floyd t-shirt is. He might even be working today.'

My cheeks heat up and I'm sure I'm blushing, but I don't move. This is like something I would have done at school—before I grew up and decided I didn't need a male to complete me. Surely I'm better than chasing after some random guy?

'What's the matter?' Kelli asks.

I draw my bottom lip between my teeth. 'I don't know, Kells. It's…'

'For goodness sakes.' She strides across the room and grabs my arm. 'Let's go already.'

She pushes me through the door to my room. 'And put on some makeup—just in case.'

I shower quickly and slip into my favourite tie-died green maxi-dress before pulling my thick, honey-gold hair into a messy bun to dry on the way. Normally that would be enough, but I heed Kelli's words and mascara my almost non-existent lashes to better highlight my cat-green eyes, then swipe on pink lip gloss before finishing the outfit off with some flat sandals.

Sending one last glance at the mirror to check I am put together, I sigh again. *What am I doing?*

'Hannah?'

'Alright, I'm coming,' I say as I grab my purse before I change my mind.

I um and ah over what we're doing the entire walk from our Darling Harbour apartment to Antonio's. Standing in front of the Italian restaurant in broad daylight, I clutch at the handle of the purse slung over my shoulder.

Kelli slips an arm through mine and leads me to a vacant table out front. 'We can at least get some lunch while you decide whether or not this guy is worth chasing down,' she says taking a seat.

I study the menu, although I don't know why. I always have the garlic prawn linguini and a garden salad. A shadow falls over the table as a waiter leans in and puts a carafe of water and two glasses between us.

'Are you ladies ready to order?' he asks.

His voice is too high to be my kiss from last night, but I glance up anyway, just to make sure. My stomach sinks a little, which surprises me. Had I really thought I would find him that easily?

I place my order before leaning back in the chair in an attempt to relax. My eyes roam the smattering of people wandering down the cobbled street, stopping occasionally to read menus, or study shop windows. It's a warm Sydney summer day, but a breeze off the nearby harbour provides some relief from the constant heat.

'And we'll have two glasses of Pino Gris,' Kelli finishes, and I half turn to find her winking at me. 'A bit of Dutch courage.'

'But I'm working later,' I protest.

'Your shift doesn't start until ten tonight. Besides, you can sleep it off this afternoon.'

There's no stopping Kelli when she's like this. I guess a little wine with lunch won't hurt. I don't have to drink the entire glass, and it'll keep Kelli happy.

When it arrives, the linguini is creamy and garlicky perfection, and the crisp white wine is the perfect accompaniment. Kelli and I chat away while we eat. With our different shift patterns, we have a week's worth of catch up to do.

An hour later we head insider to pay, having decided to forego coffee in favour of some gelato from our favourite shop on our walk home.

'Was everything to your liking, ladies?' Antonio asks as he rings up our meal.

'Perfect as always,' Kelli says, before adding, 'Hannah has something to ask you.' She nudges me in the ribs.

I send her a death stare. Antonio is waiting politely for me to speak, so I suck in some air and decide to go for it —nothing ventured nothing gained after all. 'I met a guy outside last night who was working here, and I wondered if you knew who he was.'

It sounds clumsy, and awkward to my ears, and so like a schoolgirl. Antonio's brows draw together. 'Did he do something wrong, Hannah?'

'Oh, no,' I'm quick to reassure him. I wonder how I can explain this without embarrassing myself further. 'He… uh… had on a Pink Floyd t-shirt and I'd like to buy one for my brother. I wanted to ask him where he got it.'

Kelli sniggers beside me, but I ignore her.

'Carlos,' Antonio calls, 'did we have a casual in a Pink Floyd t-shirt last night?'

Our waiter pops his head through the door from the kitchen.

'No, Pa, not that I remember.'

Antonio shrugs, 'Sorry, Hannah. Maybe he works for another place and happened to be outside here last night.'

'Thanks for asking,' I say hurriedly. 'I guess I'll have to find the t-shirt online.' I grab Kelli's hand and head for the door. 'Thanks for the lunch, it was lovely as always.'

Outside the heat hits us and we pause under the shade of the striped canopy before venturing out into the mid-day heat.

'Do you want to try the other restaurants?' Kelli asks.

I shake my head. 'I didn't really want to try this one.' As I say the words I realise they are a lie. A part of me had been hoping that Pink Floyd boy would be working today and that we were destined to meet again.

I close my eyes and take a moment to push the disap-pointment to the back of my mind. It wasn't meant to be, and no use dwelling on it.

'Come one,' I say brightly. 'Gelato's on me.'

First Date

I stand outside the restaurant, nervously tucking my hair behind my ear. This is a mistake. I turn on my heel, ready to leave, take a deep breath, and open the door, reminding myself while I was doing this—to get Kelli off my back.

Kelli had dragged me out for a drink last Friday and I reluctantly went with her, trying to drag myself out of the funk I had fallen in after my New Year's kiss.

While Kelli stood at the bar, I had caught a glimpse of a guy and my heart fluttered—New Year's guy. I had left Kelli at the bar and taken off after him. Two blocks later her turned to see who was following him, and I realised he was nothing like my kiss.

I mumbled an embarrassed apology and returned to the bar to find Kelli fuming.

'You've got to stop this,' she said after tearing a strip off me. 'The guy is gone and you need to get on with your life.'

'I am,' I mumble.

Kelli sates me down. 'Prove it to me. Go on a date with Greg.'

'What? No way.'

Greg was her brother's friend, and we'd met briefly at a bar a few months ago. I could barely remember talking to him, but I made a lasting impression in the five minutes we were in each other's company. He was persistent, to the extent of recruiting Kelli to his cause.

'You owe me one after stranding me here tonight,' she persists.

I had finally agreed and here I am, searching the restaurant for a face I barely remember. A man at a table in the back stands and waves me over. Sucking in another deep breath, I plaster on a smile and head over.

'Hannah, you look stunning,' Greg smiles, his white teeth flashing in his tanned face.

He kisses my cheek before pulling out a chair for me to sit. I stifle a cringe as his hand brushes my arm. *While I normally appreciate compliments, this is over-the-top.*

'Thank you,' I mutter as I place my bag on the floor.

Greg reaches into the ice bucket by the table and produces a bottle of Chardonnay. He tops is half-empty glass before leaning across to fill mine. I place my hand over top. 'Not for me, thanks,' I say. 'I'm not a big Chardonnay fan.'

A frown creases his brow, but he does not move the bottle away. 'This is a very good wine. I'm sure if you try it you'll enjoy it.'

Perhaps my continued resistance to the date had placed too much pressure on him, and he was overcompensating with the compliments and urging me to try the wine. Still, manners are manners. I left my hand where it was.

'Thank you, but I know what I like and what I don't.'

With the bottle hovering over my hand covered glass, I wave over a waiter with my other hand. 'Could I please have a gin and tonic, thank you.'

He takes my order and I relax, releasing the glass. As I do, Greg pours some wine into the now unprotected vessel.

'I'm sure if you try, you'll change your mind about Chardonnay,' he says, his lips pressed into a smug line, as if by putting the liquid into my glass he has won some sort of battle.

I suck in a breath and school my face into the one I use on my most annoying patients, before picking up the menu. I had chosen this Barangaroo restaurant because I thought even if the company wasn't great, the food would be.

The waiter returned with my drink, and asked if we were ready to order. I confirmed I was and Greg nods.

'We would like to start with the lobster—'

'I'm sorry, we?' I asked before he could finish.

He smiled his smug smile, which I am sure he thinks is charming but sets my teeth on edge, and say, 'I have researched the menu and critics choices online, and I believe I have put together the best dining experience for us. The food will be complimented by the Chardonnay to provide the complete dining experience.'

'Please, by all means order your perfect meal, but I am more than capable of choosing my own food,' I tell him in my best no-nonsense nurse-voice.

As he opens his mouth to protest, I turn to the waiter, who is doing his best to hide a smirk. 'I'll have the ceviche, and the pork belly with a rocket and pear side salad.'

'But...' Greg starts. I stare him down and he eventually gets the message. He orders the grilled snapper to go with his lobster main.

As the waiter turns to leave, he raises his eyebrows in query to my wine glass, and I nod. He removes the offending object as Greg takes a large mouthful of his drink, before asking, 'Are you always this difficult?'

For a moment I'm lost for words. 'Sorry?'

'I mean, I am trying to create the best dating experience I can for you, and you are fighting me at every turn.'

I stare at him, not believing what I'm hearing. He waits patiently for me to find my words. Finally I come out with, 'You believe I want you to take control and order for me?'

He nods. 'I put a lot of time curating this experience, and you haven't given any of it a chance.'

For a moment I consider whether I am in fact being difficult. No, first impressions are important, and I do not want anyone to think they can run my life. Still, he has tried, so perhaps I can afford to be a little conciliatory.

'Greg, I don't mean to be difficult. But you don't know me. You have no idea what I like or dislike.'

'I don't think that matters. I believe if you tried what I'd planned then you would enjoy the experience and widened your horizons in the process.'

I almost choke on my gin. Did he really just say that? This time the words flow out and I don't try to stop them. 'If you think I am some empty-headed chick you can mold into a better person to suit your needs, then you have the wrong girl,' I tell him, unable to keep the irritation from my voice.

At the look of hurt on his face I stop and take another sip of my drink. *Why am I here?* I wonder. *Is it so Greg can get to know me, or so he can impress me?*

'To be honest, Greg, I'm interested to know why you were so keen to ask me out when you have hardly spoken two words to me, and you know so very little about who I am.'

Greg's face is turning red, and his fingers are playing his wineglass. 'I thought… well I know something about you. You're a nurse. And I know you haven't long broken up with a long-term boyfriend. I thought maybe you might be… um… looking for the same thing as me, someone to spend your life with… and I can offer you more than nursing can… and…' He stares at his glass a moment. 'Come to think of it, I'm wondering that myself.'

Panic churns my stomach. We hardly know each other and he already thinks I'm a soul mate, or someone he can make into a soul mate. This was a mistake.

Placing my napkin on the table, I reach down and pick up my purse from the floor before standing. 'Greg, you have me pegged wrong. I think the best thing I can do for both of us is to leave before this gets any more awkward,' I say tightly.

With my head held high I walk to the bar, and our waiter wanders over to meet me. 'I would like my order to go,' I tell him.

He smiles knowingly. 'Let me tell the chef, and I'll ring that up for you.'

I keep my back to the restaurant while I wait for my food.

'Enjoy,' the waiter says, and I thank him for his help.

Down by the harbour I find a free bench and set up my picnic. The food is beautiful, as I expected it to be, and all the more delicious eating it on my own. I have almost finished the pork when my phone buzzes. Glancing down I find a message from Kelli.

What did you do to Greg? He has spent the last half hour on the phone telling Leo how rude you are?

I wait until I've finished eating before answering her.

I tried, but not my type.

:-0

Details when I get home.

What do I tell Leo?

Tell him to tell Greg he had a lucky escape ;-)

Lol.

Second Date

Darling Harbour is its normal summer weekend busy with families and friends wandering looking for somewhere to eat. I sip on my ice-cold lager and indulge in one of my favourite pastimes—people watching.

As another tour group wanders past the bar, Nate groans. 'We should have gone into the city, away from all this madness.'

Reaching across the table, I grab a couple of fries from the bowl we're sharing and drag them through the chilli sauce. I finish my mouthful before answering.

'It's close to both of us, the beer's cheaper and they do the best chilli fries.'

Nate chuckles and his grumpy frown disappears. 'True, but it's not glamorous, or romantic.'

Now it's my turn to laugh. 'I though we agreed our first date wasn't going to be either of those things, in case it turned into a red-hot mess.'

He sighs. 'I know. If it is a disaster neither of us want to lose our friendship over it.'

'Also, I'm a little cautious after my last full-on romantic date.'

I'd amused our work crowd with my Barangaroo failure yesterday over lunch, and they had empathised with me. We'd all agreed that blind dates are mostly unsatisfying.

Nate, our new registrar and lunch buddy, had confirmed this with a story about the woman his sister had set him up with the night before. She had been a nervous wreck and had drunk more than she had talked. He had ended the night by pouring her into a cab.

'Dates should be easy,' I had said, 'like going out with a friend.'

'Challenge accepted,' he quipped cheekily.

I was about to dismiss his jibe, then stopped. What if I was ignoring my friend from work, and we perhaps could have more?

'Are you serious?' I had asked instead.

He paused for a moment, coffee halfway to his mouth. 'I wasn't, but is there any reason why I shouldn't be?'

And now, here we were, having a drink after work on a trial date with rules. Alright, this was no heart stopping encounter like my New Year's guy, but the conversation was flowing, we were laughing, and I was having fun. And, I had stayed for longer than I had with Greg.

'Oh no, in your mind you're comparing this to Barangaroo guy, aren't you.' Nate says, mock shock on his face.

I snort my beer. 'OMG, how did you know?'

'The look on your face. Man, if that was how you glared at him, I'm not surprised he was straight on the phone to Kelli's brother. He probably thought you were psycho.'

'Another reason why he's no great loss. At least tonight I'm enjoying myself.'

'Good, 'cause it's your round,' he tells me.

I make my way to the bar, and half turn to watch Nate as I wait for our drinks. He is tall, and athletic and has the biggest puppy dog brown eyes. I catch the couple of girls at the table behind us eyeing him up.

He's with me ladies, I think as I carry our drinks back to the table. He turns and grins as I place the beers down, and my stomach does a little flip as my body catches on that he could *be with me*. Where has this been hiding? I haven't thought about Nate in that way before.

He reaches out and places a hand over mine. 'A penny for them?' he asks.

My face heats, my palms are sweaty, and I hope I'm not blushing. *What if he doesn't feel the same? When did this become a real date to me?*

I shrug, trying to add a lightness to my words that I'm not feeling. 'I don't know. Just thinking this is fun, I guess.'

Is it the alcohol, or are his eyes actually smouldering as he entwines his fingers through mine. 'Yes, it is,' he says.

He keeps my hand in his as he lifts his beer up. 'Here's to being more than friends.'

I clink my glass to his as the band starts playing inside.

'Want to go dance?' he asks.

I nod, and we take our drinks into the bar. Finding some standing room by a table, we aren't there for long when our tapping feet turn into movement and we hit the dance floor. At the end of the set the music slows and the band plays *Can't Help Falling in Love.*

Nate draws me into his arms and we sway to the music. Between the singers crooning and Nate's body against mine, I melt into him. Every fibre of my being is in tune with him, and he pulls me closer. A small thrill runs through me when his reaction to my body becomes obvious.

Lowering his head, he presses his lips to mine and —nothing.

I pull away and find his eyes mirror my confusion.

'But…' I say

He takes a deep breath. 'It was going so well.'

We stand in our own little bubble as everyone leaves the dance floor.

'Man,' Nate groans, and leads me outside. 'You're hot, Hannah, and I really fancy you—'

'But that kiss didn't do it for you,' I finish for him.

His laugh is hollow. 'And I respect you too much to go for something that's purely physical.'

Now it's my turn to groan. 'And I love you for that, but—'

'It's frustrating too?' He asks. His cheeky grin is back and I can't help but smile.

'Well, we tried,' I say.

Nate slips his arm through mine. 'Come on, I'll walk you home.'

'You don't have to,' I tell him. 'A couple of girls at the table behind us have been following you all night…'

Nate grimaces. 'My momma didn't bring me up that way, Hannah.'

I lean my head on his arm. 'And I appreciate that. You're going to make some girl a wonderful boyfriend.'

'And any guy would be lucky to have you,' he tells me.

My nose wrinkles. 'You know, I think I'm going to forget about dating for a while. I'm a bit over it.'

'And you need to get New Year's guy out of your head,' Nate says.

'What the?'

'You know Kelli isn't the best at keeping secrets.'

'True,' I say. 'And you're right. I need some distance between me and that kiss.'

'That must have been some kiss,' Nate chuckles.

I close my eyes, remembering New Year's guy's body against mine, the touch of his lips, the way his tongue slipped inside and I lost all sense of anything but him and I. Yep, that was some kiss.

Happy Birthday to Me

'**E**verybody else is already here,' Antonio tells me as he points me towards a table in the back. It's out of the way and set up for a birthday celebration with confetti and candles. 'There will be a band later tonight, I hope it won't spoil your party.'

'It will make the evening more fun, 'I reassure the restaurant owner before heading to my friends.

It's our little tradition to celebrate all our special occasions at Antonio's and tonight I am the guest of honour. I'm both not in the mood to do a big birthday thing, but I don't want to sit at home alone either. At least with a band tonight we can dance, and hopefully no one will notice my lack of birthday cheer.

'Happy Birthday, Hannah,' Kelli says, throwing her arms around me, before handing me a glass of sparkling wine.

Everyone stands and toasts me, then they shuffle around so I can sit beside Kelli.

'You didn't bring Nate,' she says, a single eyebrow raised.

Our out-of-sync shift patterns means we haven't had a chance to speak since the trial date.

'I think we're destined to be friends,' I tell her.

'So you don't mind if I…'

'You're incorrigible,' I laugh.

'But?'

'No, go for it,' I tell her.

I am not long seated when our banquet order starts arriving, and there is more eating than talking as we fall on the food like a pack of starving wolves. More wine flows and the band starts playing. Some of the couple in our group stand and head to the dance floor.

A while later an 80's throwback is playing and Kelli grabs my hand, 'Come on, Birthday Girl.'

She drags me up and soon we're rocking out at the edge of the crowded dance space. The song finishes, and as some of the revellers leave the floor I look up and find myself falling into a pair of cornflower blue eyes.

'One, two, one two three four.'

The music starts and I drag my gaze away.

'Toilet break,' I tell Kelli, who peels off and joins a couple of friends to carry on dancing.

I stumble to the bathroom, sit down, and try to calm my breathing. New Year's boy is a guitarist. The t-shirt, his friend saying breaks over, of course it makes sense now. And here he is, just when I have told myself to get over it—get over him. Besides, it probably meant nothing to him and *I have too much self-respect to play the groupie*, I tell myself.

Right, pep talk over, I flush the toilet and wash my hands. Staring at my flushed reflection in the mirror, I take a moment to centre myself. *Remember, you will not be a groupie!*

I open the door. The music has stopped. Damn. I stick my head out and check the hallway is clear before leaving the safety of the toilets. Someone tugs on my arm and I am pulled face to chest with a Ziggy Stardust t-shirt.

'You didn't come inside,' that deep voice I remember drawls.

I concentrate on the lightning bolt in front of me. 'I… um…'

'Couldn't get back in,' he offers.

I nod, unable to speak with his body so close to mine.

'Excuse me,' a voice says from behind. 'Woman in need of a toilet here.'

'Come with me.' He grabs by hand and leads me along the corridor, away from the restaurant and into the alley way behind.

I tug, trying to break his hold. 'Wait, hold on. What are you doing?'

'Sorting this out once and for all.'

'What?' I tear my gaze away from his chest and raise my eyes.

New Year's boy is frowning down at me, his face a picture of confusion.

'Look, New Year's boy —'

'Harry.'

'What?'

'My name is Harry.'

'Okay, Harry, what is this?'

He runs a hand through his hair. 'Since New Year, I can't seem to get…' he shakes his head. 'This is ludicrous. It was just a New Year's kiss. I mean, I don't often kiss random strangers, but you virtually fell into my arms, and… it was New Years.'

He stops talking and closes his eyes. Is he waiting for me to say something? He opens them and stares at me as if trying to read something in my face. 'Then you disappeared.' His voice is barely above a whisper.

Those eyes have me in a thrall, and heat rises from my belly at his nearness. I drag my eyes away, but I stop at those lips, and my body starts to tingle. *Get a grip, girl.*

'It was just a kiss,' I say firmly, not sure whether I'm trying to convince him or me.

Harry takes a step closer 'But was it? I can't get it out of my head. Was it the same for you, I wonder?'

I sort of nod, or is it a shake? He reaches out and as his hand touches my bare arm my skin tingles in anticipation.

'No,' I whisper, making a last-ditch attempt at holding out, but my gaze is still glued to those lips. Longing pours through me as a voice in my head tells me, *this is madness*, but every fibre of my being is willing him closer.

'If it was just a kiss,' he says, stepping in until all I can feel is the heat of his body, and his hand trailing fire down my arm as it snakes behind me and draws me to him 'Then this will only be a kiss too.'

He lowers his head, and I can't help myself. I reach up to pull his head down to mine as his hands burn a path over my back and down to my arse. My senses are overwhelmed by his touch. When our lips meet every fibre of my being explodes, melts, and then ignites again as his tongue explores my mouth.

He draws away and rests his forehead against mine, taking a moment to calm his breathing. His lips curl at the edges, and he croons, 'Oh, yes, that *was* a kiss.'

'Shut up,' I say pulling him back down for more.

Story Three: Valentine's Kiss

Take An Argument

Music throbs through my body as I move in time to the beat. I close my eyes and allow the drums and alcohol to work their magic, letting the tension of the last few days dance its way out of my body.

Nothing in Manhattan stays empty for long, and soon the floor fills. I move to the edge, happy to be alone with the music. Well, not as happy as I would be if Jason was holding me in his arms.

It was a short respite. All too soon the heat of another body presses close. There is nowhere to go, so I keep my eyes closed—blocking them out.

An arm snakes around me and my eyes fly open in time to see Alex, with his big easy smile and smoldering green eyes, dip his head as he pulls me closer. Oh no, he isn't going to—

Before I can form the thought his lips find mine and, for a fraction of a second, my body leans into his and my lips part. Then my head takes over and I push him away.

'What are you doing?' I shout over the music.

'Hey, can't shoot a man for trying,' he says, holding his hands in front in mock defense.

I turn on my heel and head back to the table, my face flushed with anger. Aaron and Jess are so deep in conversation, I don't think they even noticed we were gone.

'Hey,' fingers wrap around my arm. I half turn towards Alex, then pull away. 'No need to bother them with this,' he says, taking his seat.

Staring at his profile, a multitude of emotions rage in my head. Thing is, I had enjoyed flirting with Alex. I was flattered he found me attractive. Then the guilt welled up, and I took myself off to the dance floor to reset. How was I to know he would take it as an invitation and not only follow me, but try to kiss me?

First kisses are special, and this one—what little there was off it—was no different. My body still tingles with electricity, and the promise of more than a kiss. No! He's a potential client. This isn't right.

'I'm sorry,' I mumble as I grab my coat and bag. 'I have to go.'

I pull the duvet over my head and groan silently. It was nothing in the grand scheme of things—an almost kiss at the most. I roll over and stare at Jason's face.

His dark lashes form quarter moons on his pale face, curls of black hair almost obscuring them. I reach out a hand and curl a finger in a lock, smiling at the contrasts of my dark skin and his pale complexion.

He opens his eyes, blinks a couple of times to focus before he smiles back. 'How did the schmoozing go last night? Are you on the team?'

I catch my bottom lip between my teeth, sure my guilt must be written over my face. He captures my hand in his, planting a kiss on my palm, suspecting nothing.

'I don't know. I guess I'll find out today,' I tell him. 'The fact Aaron invited me out with them… well, it's promising.'

He kisses my hand again. 'I'm sure you're a shoe in, and we'll celebrate tonight.'

My brows draw together, and my mouth goes dry. What have I forgotten now? 'Tonight? What's tonight?'

Jason abruptly releases my hand and turns a cold gaze on me. I wrack my brain but I can't think of anything. I've been so wrapped up pitching the project with Aaron, I've literally lost track of time.

'It's February the 14th,' Jason prompts, raising an eyebrow. 'Valentine's Day?'

Slowly it dawns on me. We don't normally celebrate the day of romance, but for some reason this year he wants to take me to a swanky new restaurant his friends have been raving about.

I suspect the dinner is to soften me up and convince me we should buy a house together. Maybe he thinks being around other couples will show me this commitment thing isn't so bad.

'Oh,' I say, 'of course. Dinner at La Mange. I didn't forget,' I say as I swing my legs out of bed.

In the mirror I see him propped on an elbow as I search for something to wear. 'You won't be late, will you? I mean, we haven't spent much time together lately, and I'm looking forward to a night out with you.'

My lips curl into a smile. In spite of the commitment anxiety gnawing at my stomach, I'm looking forward to an evening with Jason too. The chance to talk about something other than construction, and to be with someone I can be myself with—priceless

'And, while we're eating, maybe we can look through some of the houses Jayne's found for us.'

And Just like that my happy feelings disappear. 'I told you, I'm still so busy at work, I don't want to commute. I mean it's ok for you. You're either away chasing a story, or you're at home writing it.'

The moment the words leave my mouth I'm sorry for them. No, that's not quite true. I meant the words, I didn't mean to sound so… angry. I make my way to the bed and lay out my suit and blouse before sitting down beside Jason.

'Look, I'm sorry. I know you're excited about being able to buy our own place, but I'm just not ready for it.'

Jason rolls onto his back, and threads his fingers behind his head, deliberately not looking at me.

'And you know how I feel, Cassandra. We can't say like this forever. I want more in my life—in our lives— than work. I thought you wanted that too.'

'I do.' I take a deep breath. 'Do we have to do this now. I have a big meeting this morning…'

Jason sighs. 'We can't keep putting this off, Cass. At some point we need to lay our cards on the table, and tonight is it.'

I remain still. Jason has started this conversation numerous times over the last month, and every time we do I feel like I am being backed into a corner. I put him off, hoping it will all go away, wanting to keep things as they are.

Pushing myself off the bed I pad to the bathroom. As I reach for the handle Jason says, 'Please be at the dinner at seven tonight.'

'I'll try,' I tell him. 'But if I get—'

'If you're not there then I will take it you have decided that you and I want different things.'

My fingers grip the door handle, my knuckles showing white. He can't mean that, can he?

Mixed With Anger

After my great start to the day, my morning spiraled further downwards. I miss my train, then there's a line at the coffee shop and the project meeting had started by the time I make it into the office.

I loathe being unprepared. Being a woman in the construction game is bad enough. Being a black woman, well let's just say it adds another level of hard. I have to work longer and harder just to be accepted, let alone appreciated, for my abilities.

So, when I slip into the meeting late fumbling with my messenger bag and coffee, I am completely out of sorts.

Aaron snipes, 'Pleased you could make it, Cassandra,' as I take my seat, and I grimace at his censure.

I mumble an apology as I take my laptop and project file from my bag. Aaron is just finishing the project vision slides, and pulls up the cost and project schedules section. 'And I will now hand over to Cassandra to talk you through the details.'

Fortunately I'd had time on the train to review my part of the presentation. Aaron passes me the clicker and I allow myself a moment for my gaze to range around the table before starting. Alex is sitting beside Aaron, and he gives me a nod of encouragement.

I blush, remembering last night, then turn away. Now is not the time to be distracted by whatever this is with Alex, or what happened this morning for that matter. I put on my business face and begin.

'We have a savings share scheme with all our contractors to focus them on coming in or under budget,' I tell the group as I finish up talking through the figures. I'm in my element. I am good at my job. I work hard to be the best, but so far I've only been given responsibility for initial development costings and scheduling. This time I want to see a development through as the Project Manager, and I aim to impress.

Throughout the presentation Alex and his partners ask questions, and I have answers for all of them until one of them asks Aaron, 'You're proposing to use Ms Jamieson as Project Manager, has she ever done anything this big before?'

Aaron rakes his hand across his beard. We prepared two answers for this question, depending on how the room is reading. The first is a more experienced project manager will oversee the project and I will shadow them. The second is to explain that last year I assisted on a large development, and it was only through my efforts we kept on track.

Of course, I prefer the second option, but I am prepared for both. Aaron catches my eye and smiles, and I know he is going to back me.

'I believe Cassandra has what it takes to bring this project in on time and on budget,' he finishes. 'Is there anything else?'

Alex closes his folder and makes eye contact with each of his colleagues, checking where they're at. Finally, he smiles.

'Right, we have an agreement in principle. Of course, our lawyers will have to cross the t's and dot the i's over the next few days, but I don't think that prevents us breaking out the champaign and celebrating tonight.'

The elation I had felt moments ago sours. Being part of the team will mean socialising, and working evenings, and I am going to have to say no. How will Alex take that? As a rejection of him? Or, worse still, as a lack of commitment to the project?

Alex's voice breaks through my panic. 'Cassandra, you haven't said anything. Do you have plans for tonight?'

The dread turns to resentment, then anger. Why am I even second guessing this? It's my big chance, and I can't blow it but being different.

'Um, nothing I can't put off until a little later,' I assure him.

'Oh, I thought maybe it might be a Valentine's thing,' Alex sniggers, and others join him—because obviously no one in their right mind celebrates Valentine's Day.

While everyone packs up, I pull out my phone and text: Something's come up. Can we push things back an hour?

I wait for the dots to tell me Jason is responding. Nothing. I know he's working on an article at home today, so why isn't he answering?

'Is there a problem?' Alex asks, but in a way that sounds like he expects me to make any issues go away so his plans can go ahead. From where he stands by the door he can see my phone, and I quickly gather it up. I don't want him knowing about my private life. Not just because of the kiss, or the flirting—but because work is work, and home is home.

'Ah... no,' I tell him. 'Just fixing a scheduling conflict.'

His face splits into that lazy grin, and my stomach churns. How had I ever thought this man anything other than smarmy?

And A Touch of Angst

Back in my office I set up my laptop and plonk into the chair, before swinging round to stare out at the New York skyline. I'm a project manager, I should be able to sort reschedule this evening and make everything work.

I turn back to my desk and my gaze fixes on the collage of photos under my screen. Usually the images of Jason and I lifts my spirits, reminding me of what I'm working for on those days when everything seems too hard. Today they remind me that I should be making more time to be with him.

I open the contract request document. I have to get this drawn up and to Aaron for his approval before I leave today. Out of the corner of my eye, I catch sight of the photo of Jason and me at our college ball.

It was out third date, and our first kiss. I still remember the tentative touch of his lips as we swayed to some song

I can't even remember. What I do remember is he tasted of lemon and wine, and smelled of sandalwood. And that when he pulled me closer and the kiss deepened that my body awakened and I couldn't get close enough to him—how I'd wished we were somewhere else so we could do more than kiss.

A smile tugs at my lips. The following weekend we went camping—alone. The selfie we took with the mountains in the background was our one moment out of the tent. After out first time, lying on top of sleeping bags, Jason had leaned over and taken my face in his hands.

'You are so beautiful,' he told me. 'Every time I look at you my heart sings.' He'd brushed his lips against mine and my body tingled from head to toe, and that kiss was all it took to ignite the fires again.

'Um, sorry, Cassandra, you were miles away.'

With great reluctance I return from the wilderness to find Liz, the graduate I time share with two other Project Managers, standing by my desk.

'Yes?'

'I'm doing a coffee run. Do you want anything?'

'Yes, please.' I reach into my bag for some cash. 'A double shot. I'm finding it difficult to concentrate on the legal stuff.'

Liz grins, perhaps sensing an opportunity. 'If you need any help…,' she offers before departing.

I follow her progress as she heads for the elevators. I add a task on my to-do list to review the project plan and see if there is anything I can assign to Liz—after all, Aaron had done the same for me and I wouldn't be here without him.

My pen hovers, remembering the week Aaron assigned me as administrator on one of his projects. Anxious for everything to be perfect, I rang Jason to tell him I needed to work late Friday finishing up the initial documents, then be in early Monday to go over them before meeting with the client.

Jason had been excited until he realized we would have to change our weekend plans to drive down Friday evening to his parent's then back Monday morning. We had our first major argument. We had not long moved in together and wanted to introduce me to his family.

'So, what are you saying? You want me to cancel?'

Yes, my head said, but my mouth went, 'Nooo…' Families really weren't my thing at all, not even my own, but I knew this was important to Jason. 'Perhaps we can leave early tomorrow, and come back late Sunday.'

'Cass—'

'I know that doesn't give us as much time, but I can't mess this up, Jase. I have been working so hard for this.'

The line was silent for a long time, and I could imagine the hurt on his face.

'Alright. I'll give them a call.'

He'd hung up, and when I arrived home around 11 that night, he was already asleep—or at least pretending to be. When the alarm rang at 5 the next morning, I packed and was ready to go by 5:30.

The atmosphere in the car as I gulped my wake up coffee had been tense. Eventually I caved and said, 'If you're mad at me, tell me. Don't do this passive aggressive thing.'

'Is this what our life together is going to be like? You putting work before us? Before me?' His tone was bitter and his hands gripped the wheel hard enough to turn his knuckles white.

Anger bubbled, but I still tried for a reasonable response. Should I point out my ambition was something he always said attracted him? Or should I tell him meeting his family scares the hell out of me?

Either of those would have been preferable to what I actually said.

'I might have known you'd play the victim card. Have you any idea how much harder it is for me to take a single step forward at work? How much more I have to do to be noticed when other people with less experience are given opportunities I'm not.'

'You mean people like me—white, middle class, males?' he spits. 'Are we back there again?'

'Yes, because you might be able to ignore it when you want, but it's always there for me.'

Oppressive silence fills the car, sucking the joy from the drive. All I can think about is, this whole relationship thing with him will never work. We are too different.

He grew up in happy family suburbia where his mom and dad still live, and everyone comes home for the holidays. After four years working for major newspapers, he had built a good enough reputation to go freelancing and was making a good living. How can I make him understand that when he walks into a room he is seen —I'm not.

And then he had swept all those fears away.

'I get it, you know.' His voice is so quiet, she almost doesn't hear him. 'That Democrats rally I covered last week—if it weren't for mainstream media having quotas, all the reporters would have been different versions of me.'

My heart thaws a little, but Jason isn't finished.

'It's just…I can understand but still be annoyed when you don't put us first.'

I smile warily. My turn to give a little. 'If, I'm honest, the family thing is hard for me, and I may have been looking for a way out,' I say.

After my father walked out, my mother was so intent on providing for my brother and I she left us in the care of her mother. She went on to build a successful business, but still did not make time for her children.

Once gran died, the glue holding our family together was gone. My brother moved to London, and I spoke to him perhaps once or twice a year. My monthly lunches with my mother were more like business meetings. So far, I had avoided revealing my relationship with Jason. Given her lectures on men versus career—like they were two separate options—I couldn't face her disappointment.

Jason reaches out and places a hand over mine. 'I know. But if you and I are going to make a go of this, we need to find a mid-way.'

I nod, unable to speak. Tears well in my eyes, and I choke. Should I be with someone who wants a traditional family life? For so long it has been me and my ambition. Still, when I'm with Jason I believe anything is possible, and that I am the best version of myself. I can't give that up.

We arrive at his parents place as the sun is coming up. Jason opens the trunk and retrieves our bags. I meet him at the back of the car.

'Wait,' I say.

He drops the bags on the ground and stares at me expectantly.

I reach up and entwine my fingers in the hair curling at the nape of his neck. 'You are a good man, and I love you very much. I want to be with you and I'll try to do better.'

I rise on tiptoes and kiss him on the cheek.

He leans his forehead on mine and says, 'I will also try to be more understanding of the different pressures you face.'

He wraps his arms around me, a cheeky grin forming on his lips. 'Now, we have just had our first major fight, and it can't be said to be over until we kiss and make up.'

With that, he lowers his lips to mine and, at their touch, my mouth parts. His tongue slips inside, gently probing my mouth. My body melts into his as a heat begins to rise in the pit of my stomach, spreading outwards threatening to engulf me.

He draws me closer and his hands range down my back, coming to a halt on my butt. I can feel how much he wants me, and my body responds.

'Ahem.'

We freeze, and turn as one towards the house where, we find a Jason duplicate standing on the porch grinning.

'Welcome home little bro. I surely hope that's your girlfriend, and not some stray you picked up on the way.'

I must have turned beet red and could barely face him all weekend. When we arrived back in New York, Jason's brother had sent the photo he had snuck of our first makeup kiss, and it is still one of my favorites in the collage.

I've tried hard, I tell the photo, but I still haven't found the balance. Until I do, how can I make more of a commitment?

As if on cue, my phone pings. It's Jason texting back: You're kidding, right? It was hard enough to get this booking on Valentine's Day.

Add A Splash Of Over~Accommodation

I press send. The contract request has gone to Aaron for review. I check the time on my computer—4:15. Fingers crossed Aaron will have time to review it before he leaves today.

Standing, I stretch to relieve the pressure in my neck and shoulders that has been building all day. If I leave at 5, I can get to the bar, stay for an hour or so and show willing, and still be at the restaurant in time to meet Jason.

Ping. I turn to see who is Teams messaging me.

Aaron: Can you come over and we can go through this together?

I sigh. I should have guessed. To compress timescales my mentor prefers to have any questions dealt with as he reads a document, making changes as he goes.

Me: On my way.

The cubicles main office is emptying as I open Aaron's door.

'Ah, good. I've told legal to expect this tonight so they can work on it this weekend,' Aaron says as I shut the door before joining him at the conference table dominating his corner office.

Two hours later I stand and grab my jacket off the back of the chair. We're done.

'I'll just send this to legal and meet you by the elevators. Hopefully the others have left some champagne for us.'

I check my phone. 6:30. Damn it. I can pop my head in at the bar, have a drink, then head to the restaurant. I'll be 15…20 minutes late at the most.

I pack everything as fast as I can and make my way through the deserted floor. Pressing the call button, I resist the urge to tap my foot with impatience. Where is Aaron?

The doors open and I duck inside to press the hold button, gnawing my bottom lip as the minutes tick down and Aaron still doesn't appear.

Finally he emerges, pulling on his coat as he walks towards the open door. Punching the button as soon as he enters, I relax. It will be a small drink and half an hour late.

The bar is crowded with couples, but Aaron and I manage to push our way through to the back, where our newly formed project team has a table.

Alex stands to make way for us, ensuring that I am sitting beside him. He smiles and leans in close to my ear. 'Pleased you could make it. I'm so looking forward to many more evenings together as this development progresses.'

My stomach sinks and I pull away, suddenly wary of this charming man. Am I only on this project because he's into me? How will he handle that when he finds out I'm not interested?

The pleasure I had felt at being attractive to someone other than Jason has turned sour. I check my phone as Alex pours me some bubbles from the bottle chilling on the table. 6:45. I take a sip and relax as the sharp, fruity liquid slides down my throat.

Turning away from Alex, I join the others, allowing my excitement about our development that will transform a tired old shopping center into a vibrant community space reign for the first time today.

My glass is almost empty when Alex leans in to top it off. I place my hand over top and he frowns, and he slides an arm along the back of my chair.

'We can always leave these guys and go somewhere more private,' he says, staring deep into my eyes.

I fight back a gag reflex. What had I been thinking last night? I had been flattered to be with some of the city's movers and shakers. And I had been attracted to the confidence and power Alex exuded, and he was certainly not bad to look at. But how had I missed the predatory look in his eye?

My phone vibrates. I glance at the screen 7:10. Where are you?

'What do you say?' Alex's voice is close to my ear.

I'm frozen in place until Aaron turns. His eyes drift across the message on my phone and he turns to me.

'Cassandra, it's been so good of you to come in for a drink when you had other plans. You head off now, and I'll get in the next bottle. I just hope we haven't made you too late.'

I have never felt so grateful for my mentor and his support than I did at that moment—except perhaps when he swings my chair around, giving me the room to escape without having to face Alex.

'Good night everyone,' I say as I gather my things.

Aaron escorts me to the door. Outside he places a hand on my arm. 'We need to be careful, Cassie. Alex has a reputation, and I wouldn't like you to think we expect you to play nice with him if he makes you feel uncomfortable.'

I squeeze Aaron's hand. 'Thank you,' I say.

'No, thank you for all the hard work you put in on this bid. Now, go, enjoy your evening.'

As he disappears back into the bar I attempt to hail a taxi, but they're all occupied. I set out at a brisk walk, hoping I'm not too late.

As I rush to the restaurant, I contemplate what I'll say to Jason. Am I ready to focus on something other than my career? I'm not sure, but perhaps there is a compromise I haven't thought of yet—perhaps a commitment to buy a house next year?

To Ruin A Relationship

I frantically search the crowded restaurant for Jason before pulling out my phone.

Where are you?

I got your message, you're not ready for us. I'm at the apartment packing. Will be gone in half an hour.

OMG!

The glass of wine I had threatens to resurface as his words hit me. Jason is moving out. Just like that.

'Are you okay, miss?' A concerned waiter touches my arm. 'Can I get you some water, or something?'

I blink a couple of times and take in the scene around me. I'm standing at the front of the line waiting to be seated, and everyone is staring at me.

'Um, no, sorry. I've gotta go.' I push past him and head for the door.

Outside the evening air hits me, clearing my head somewhat. I hastily flag down a taxi. This time the gods are with me, and within seconds I am heading home. I make the driver let me off at the Bodega on the corner.

They don't have champagne, but they do have an alright Prosecco. I grab a bunch of flowers that have perhaps seen better days, and make my way to the counter. And there I see it, the perfect accessory for my plan.

I pay, praying this little diversion hasn't made me too late. Minutes later I am home. Although I fumble with my keys, I manage to open the external door without dropping anything—a miracle in my flustered state. The elevator will take too long, so I rush up the stairs, arriving at our fourth floor apartment shaking and breathing heavily as the door opens.

Jason fills the space, duffle bag flung over his shoulder. His eyes widen in surprise when he sees me, before slipping to the goods I have in my arms.

'If you think some wilted offering will make up for standing me up when I explained how important to night was to me, then you are wrong,' he tells me, his voice all controlled fury.

'Please, Jason, just give me a moment.' I plead, hoping I haven't broken things irreparably.

He takes a deep breath. 'Okay, but tell me something first. Is this all about work, or is there someone else?'

Heat rushes to my cheeks and I realize they must have colored when Jason's face hardens and he turns to brush past me.

No. I will not let it end like this. I stand my ground. I thrust the flowers and wine at him and he has no option but to take them, or let them crash to the floor.

And there, in the dingy, low-lit hallway, with Jason now clutching my rather sad Valentine's gift, I let it all out.

'One of the project team has been paying me a lot of attention. He did kiss me, and I was flattered.' I make myself absorb the hurt on Jason's face, because he deserved me acknowledging that.

'I could tell you I let it go to far as a rebellion against you pushing the house idea, but that would only be part of the truth. In all honesty, I have been so caught up in this project, and the need to prove myself at work, that I got carried away and I forgot about what is import to me.'

I stare at the floor. It's now or never I tell myself. But before I can speak, Jason says, 'This is where you tell me that we are the most important thing, and you expect me to believe it while you ask for me to wait until you are ready.'

Even though he is angry, I can't help but smile. 'Ah, how well you know me. And yes, that is what I was going to tell you over dinner.'

Jason sighs. 'Same old—'

'Then, when I arrived, you were gone.' I rush on, because if I don't get this out now I'm afraid I never will. 'When you weren't there it hit me. My life is nothing without you. You are the sunshine and light to my grey darkness.'

'True, but—'

I look up at him and capture his eyes, and beseech him. 'Please, let me finish. This is difficult enough as it is.'

He hesitates then nods. 'Alright, go ahead. Let's get this over with.'

At that moment I understand that explaining my point of view will not work. It's time to lay it all on the line— to prove I want to change.

I reach into my pocket, pull out my special purchase and go down on one knee.

'Jason, for such a long time I have tried to believe that you and I are two individuals who happen to be together. I have resisted all your efforts to make us a family, only to realize that we already are one. I know when I pull away I hurt you again and again. So this time I am taking a step towards you—towards us. I love you more than life itself, and I will give everything else up, even my job, if you will only stay and marry me. ' I hold out the lime green candy ring, unable to meet Jason's eyes.

I expect to be met with a no. Or a sigh. Or even silence. What I don't expect is clapping. I raise my head to find our neighbors at the top of the stairs, silly grins plastered to their faces, clapping.

I smile sheepishly as Jason pulls me to my feet and into our apartment. Placing my Valentine's gifts on the side table, he drops his bag to the floor and slips mine off my shoulder before hanging it on the coat rack. I push the door shut with my foot.

'You know you just took a step beyond buying a house together?' he asks.

After my big declaration, words seem to have deserted me, so I nod.

'You know, if I stay, I'm going to hold you to that proposal, and there will be a huge family wedding?'

A little bubble of hope forms in my stomach, but I am too scared to let it loose. I nod again.

A wicked gleam sparkles in Jason's eyes as he steps towards me, 'And we will still be looking at houses?'

I open my mouth to object, but stop myself. Really, would it be so bad living out of the city and spending more time together? Or would I rather spend my evenings with the likes of Alex?

'Okay,' I say.

Jason smiles, a goofy happy grin and says, 'Then I accept your proposal.'

He reaches out a hand and I slip the candy ring into my pocket as I take it. He frowns. 'Oh no, my lovely, this is for you to slip the ring on.'

I laugh giddily and place the ring on his finger. Jason admires it like it was at the most expensive diamond, then pulls me into his arms.

'So, feel like running yet?' he asks.

I stop and take stock. At every new step in our relationship I have fought feelings of being caged in, of being turned into something I don't want to be. This time, making the ultimate commitment, that cage has evaporated.

I grin stupidly. 'What I am is deliriously happy.'

His body relaxes as he pulled me into his arms. As his head dips I raise my lips and meet his full on. The happiness bubble explodes inside me as every fibre of my being connects with him. The fire in my belly ignites and I lose track of everything else as I wrap my arms around him and hold him like I'll never let him go.

Story Four:
Easter Kiss

Easter Egg Hunt

Joe shuffles his feet impatiently as I stand in front of the wooden door, hand poised to knock.

'C'mon, mum. Everyone else'll be there already.' His voice is plaintive.

When you're seven you don't worry about feeling awkward as the only single parent. All you want is to join your friends hunting easter eggs, then gorging on them until you bring on a sugar coma.

'Mum! They'll start without me!'

Sighing, I pick up the brass knocker and let it fall. The door immediately opens, revealing a short, slightly plump woman, a large grin on her face.

'Great, I thought we'd have a riot on our hands if we held the hunt off any longer. Joe, the others are on the patio.'

Joe didn't need to be told twice. As he dashed off to join his friends, our hostess linked her arm through mine and led me in the opposite direction.

'Abbie, I need a hand in the kitchen.'

As my oldest and dearest friend, Cathy was aware I dreaded school get togethers. Being a single parent in a small village was bad enough. It was worse still when you've been to school with at least one parent of each child. Everyone knew my "tragic" tale. The few that hadn't were soon filled in on how my husband died in an accident racing to the hospital to be there for Joe's birth.

The modern kitchen would have been an anomaly in a country cottage, but it had been sympathetically done to blend the new with the old. It featured on Cathy's website promoting her interior design business, winning her lots of work.

The granite bench tops were laden with homemade mini-pies, sausage rolls, canapés, assorted cakes, with a smattering of fruit skewers, crudité and dips.

'I see Mark's been busy,' I say.

'Indeed,' Cathy smiles. 'Sometimes being married to the local baker has its perks.' She grimaces and runs a hand over her hips. 'Although, sometimes I think the perks may not be worth it.'

I laugh. 'You're gorgeous,' I'm still stick thin and have always envied her curves. 'I guess we all want what we haven't got.'

'This sounds serious,' a cheerful voice interrupts.

I turn to find Mark, Cathy's husband, opening the fridge and removing a couple of bottles of Prosecco.

'Time to bring on the food, I think. If you leave it any longer half the parents will be blotto before the hunt is over,' he says as he heads back outside.

Cathy's eyes twinkle. 'That's a tempting idea.'

I laugh. 'Oh no you don't. The last time that happened I got stuck with Essie confessing to me that she and Adam were not having regular sex, and did I think that was normal? I've never been so embarrassed.'

Cathy is almost doubled over with laughter. 'And then she announced to the whole room that you were probably the only person here who'd had sex in the last six months.'

'I was mortified,' I say, tears streaming down my cheeks.

'Not as mortified as Adam. He couldn't wait to get her home fast enough.'

I wiped the tears from my cheeks. 'She turned up to school pick up the next day looking like the cat who got the cream, so perhaps it worked out for her. C'mon, we'd better get the food out.'

I walk around the central island to the sink to wash my hands, catching my reflection in the window as I did. With my chocolate-brown eyes and long black hair, I couldn't have been more different from my blue-eyed, blonde-haired bubbly friend. It's not that I obsess about my looks, but I've always felt a little in Cathy's shadow.

Reaching for a towel I dry my hands as I watch the kids hunting through the bushes for Easter eggs. Mark is filling the glasses of the group of parents under the shade of ancient oak tree in the centre of the garden. I stand on tiptoes, trying to plot the quickest route to the food table when my eyes fall on an attractive, dark haired man. For a moment my heart stops beating.

I turn on my heel and glared at Cathy. 'Is that Greg?'

'Oh, yeah, he arrived last night,' Cathy says, placing mini-pies on an oven tray.

'And you didn't think to tell me?' My voice is stiff with tension.

Cathy glances up. 'Oh Abbie, surely you don't still hold a grudge after all these years?'

'You mean have I forgiven the guy that made my high school years miserable? The guy who either ignored me completely, or criticised everything I did? Remember when he lectured me outside class about going away for a weekend with my boyfriend just before exams?'

Cathy's eyebrows arch. 'I guess you haven't then. Look, he's changed. Even he and Mark are getting on better. '

I glance out the window, scanning the crowd. 'Where's his latest girlfriend?'

Over the years Mark had kept us updated with his older brother's movements. The tales usually involved some new super-building project in an exotic location, or attending swanky parties with a beautiful model-type on his arm.

'I think he's single at the moment,' Cathy says as she slides the pies into the oven. 'Why? Are you interested?'

I almost drop the dip I'm opening. 'Hardly. How long do I have to endure his presence for?'

'He's opening up his own practice restoring and renovating heritage buildings.'

Her voice fades as memories flood my mind. The first time we met the school football hero Greg hadn't even acknowledged my existence. Soon after he sauntered past my locker and said, 'Hey you're Mark's friend, aren't you? I saw you out with Carl Latimer last night. You should stick to painting, you'll get more out of it than you will from him.'

Then there was the last time I spoke to him. I was waiting for Carl outside the movie theatre in Portsmouth. A car pulled up to the curb and the window went down. I studiously ignored it, wishing Carl would hurry up.

'Abbie, what are you doing out here alone?'

I screwed up my eyes to get a better view. 'Greg?'

'Of course, it's Greg. Who'd you think... do you need a lift home?'

'I thought you were at Uni?'

'What? I leave tomorrow. Hop in, I'll take you home.'

'I'm going to the movies with Carl.'

'I don't know what you see in that numpty. He should've picked you up from home, not left you waiting in the cold.'

At that moment I agreed with Greg. I was cold and fed up. And why hadn't Carl picked me up? Some half-arsed excuse about it being quicker to get here if he didn't have to swing by my house after football. But his game had finished ages ago.

'Get in and I'll take you home,' Greg urged.

I moved towards the car, thinking perhaps it would be for the best, when I saw Carl crossing the road.

'It's okay, he's here,' I said, relief running through me.

'You make sure you give that prat an earful for making you wait,' Greg said as he drove off.

'Who was that?' Carl asked as he joined me.

'Just Greg,' I said.

Carl frowned and snarled. 'What a wanker, trying to pick you up when I'm not around.'

'He wasn't… he was just…' Carl's face was so twisted in anger I couldn't find the words to defend Greg. Not wanting to start an argument, I said, 'Let's go and watch the movie.' I led the way into the theatre.

Now the guy who felt he had the right to tell me how to live my life was back—for good.

Avoiding Small Talk

'Abbie. Abbie, hello,' the voice follows me as I carry the tray of dips out to the patio.

Putting my load down, I bite back a sigh and plaster a smile on my face. 'Hi Essie.'

'Abbie. I'm so pleased you made it. I've been meaning to apologise to you—'

'Essie, we've known each other for years. No apologies necessary. Let's just forget it ever happened.'

Essie face flushes to the roots of her red hair. 'Oh, but I must. I mean… how insensitive… to actually suggest… I'm mortified.'

And here we go again. Poor widowed Abigail. We must treat her with kid gloves. I want to yell "It's been seven years, give it a rest already." Or, even worse, "You know, he left me the day he died."

I don't though, because some of these people were Carl's friends. Not only are they still grieving, but word would get back to Carl's parents and that would strain our already rocky relationship.

Only Cathy and Mark know that Carl was spending more and more time away from home during my pregnancy. And that the morning before he died, he told me he wasn't ready for a child and he was leaving me.

They were there supporting me when I gave birth to Joe. They are the only ones who know Carl was not killed racing back to be by my side, but texting me he hoped the birth went well and he'd call tomorrow.

Oh, how I wish I could tell each and every one of them what a monumentally selfish wanker Saint Carl was.

'Here, mum.' Joe holds out his easter bag full of goodies. 'Can you hold these for me?'

I smile down at the boy who looks so much like his father, and I know that for his sake I will never utter those words.

'Sure, hon.' I take the bag and he dashes off, all carefree energy and sunshine.

'He's growing so big,' Essie says. 'My Samantha is so tiny, she could pass for a pre-schooler.'

'She'll catch up soon, they always do,' I assure her as I scan the backyard to see who is here… only to find Greg watching me. My heart does an unexpected flip and I quickly avert my gaze.

'Essie, Cathy should have a couple of trays of hot food ready, want to help me bring them out?'

'Sure,' she smiles, heartbreakingly pleased to have been asked, reminding me of the shy girl she used to be at school—always hanging around, but never really part of anything.

With the three of us working the food was soon served, and there was no reason not to join the party. I trail Cathy and Essie outside, preparing myself for a couple of hours of mindless chatting and gossip.

I avoid the group standing by the table. Essie's husband is at the centre, and that man does not know how to keep his hands to himself. His presence reminds me there are worse things than being single. I join Cathy and Mark under the oak tree, pleased for the shade and a vantage point that allows me to keep an eye on Joe without seeming to.

'It's all going well so far.' Mark beams. 'The kids are hyped on chocolate.' He gestures to the group playing football down the other end of the garden. 'And the parents are getting pleasantly merry on bubbles and punch.'

'Yes,' I agree, 'this is the party sweet spot. I give it another hour and the kids'll be fighting.'

Cathy laughs. 'Or the parents.'

I sip my drink, my eyes wandering round the yard, stopping on the group of parents watching the kids play football. One is semi-refereeing, more to make sure everyone is included than to impose rules. My eyes widen. Greg is down there. I never thought kids were his thing.

He turns to talk to, is that Tony? Ah, those two were thick as thieves at school. Tony raises a hand and waves. I smile in return just as Greg turns his head, catching the last of my smile, and he smiles back. My stomach flips as a group of boys almost topple him over in their enthusiasm to get the ball. *Stop it*, I tell my treacherous body, *I will not have you lusting after my high school nemesis*. I take another mouthful of drink and find myself sucking on ice.

'Let me get you another,' Cathy offers.

'No, you stay and relax,' I tell her. 'I saw the other pitchers in the fridge. I'll bring one out.'

'Thanks, Abs. Remember red for non-alcoholic.'

The kitchen is cool and blessedly empty, perfect to work out why that smile from Greg set my heart fluttering. I place the pitcher on the counter before turning to close the fridge door. As it swings shut, I come face to face with Joe, tears silently tracing their way down his cheeks, wrapped in the arms of—Greg?

'Hey, mum, Joe took a bit of a fall and has skinned his knee,' Greg's familiar voice informs me, and I am no longer calm. 'He's been very brave, but I think a tidy up and band-aid might be in order.'

Greg's blue eyes twinkle and he winks conspiratorially when I finally get the courage to look at his face. Although my heart is beating rapidly, I catch on—play this low key.

'OK, pop him up on the bench and I'll get the first aid kit,' I say, my voice sounding oddly breathless.

Get a grip, it's only a scratch, I tell myself as I reach for the kit I know Cathy keeps in the pantry, all the while knowing it's Greg presence, not Joe's injury that's thrown me off balance.

I turn, expecting Greg to have left, only to find him handing Joe a lolly from the stash in the bowl on the bench.

'This is going to sting,' I warn Joe before dabbing the antiseptic wipe over his knee. A couple of the scratches are quite deep, but he's had worse. I cover the wound with a dressing and give him a hug. 'All done,' I say, helping him down.

'Thanks, mum.' He heads for the door, ready to return to his friends, before half turning and asking, 'Are you coming, Greg?'

Greg's face split with a grin. 'In a moment, mate. I'm just going to have a drink, then I'll be back.'

I busy myself repacking the first aid kit to hide my shaking hands.

'He'll be fine,' Greg reassures me as he reaches past me for a glass and pours himself a drink. I am hyper-aware of his presence.

'He's a good kid.'

'I know,' I snap, annoyed he has taken it on himself to reassure me. Why is it he always manages to irritate me? 'I'm sorry, these get togethers always wind me up. Thank you for bringing Joe in.'

I raise my head. Greg is staring at me with a strange, almost tender look in his eyes. Everything slows down. The air between us feels heavy and I find myself leaning towards him.

Then, without even seeming to move, Greg's lips are on mine. A whisper touch at first, but as I respond he takes that as encouragement and I sense his hunger. The world goes dark, my body glows and comes alive for the first time in I can't remember when. I ache with need and I want so much to reach up and tangle my fingers in Greg's dark, curly hair. A moan escapes my lips and I'm about to wrap my arms around him when I hear footsteps in the hall. All of a sudden my lips are released.

I slowly open my eyes to find myself alone, my heart beating so fast I think I might have a heart attack. *What the hell was that?*

'Abs, are you okay?' Cathy's voice comes from the hallway.

'Yes,' I mumble. 'Just coming.'

Early Morning Visit

I roll over, open my eyes and try to focus on the bedside clock. 7:30! I flop back onto the pillows trying to figure out what had woken me. There it is. Is that Transformer music? No, it can't be. Joe knows he has to ask if he can watch TV before breakfast.

I groan. It must be all that sugar yesterday. He's normally such a good kid. I slip into my slippers, running fingers through my hair as I head downstairs. I stop halfway down. There's a male voice in the living room, and it isn't Optimus Prime.

I rush down the last few steps and fling open the door to find Joe curled up on the sofa, leaning against... Greg?

'What the h—'

'Sorry Abbie, we tried not to wake you,' Greg grins up at me as if it's perfectly normal for him to be watching TV with my son at 7:30 in the morning.

'Tried not to wake me?' I force out between gritted teeth. 'What in the… what are you doing here?' I finally manage to ask, in quite a normal voice I think, until Joe looks up in surprise.

'Sorry, mum. I forgot. I invited Greg for pancakes this morning,' he says, his little face so earnest, pleading with me not to show him up. 'He helped me yesterday… and I thought…'

I stare at Joe. He's never done anything like this before, and I don't know what to say. A gamut of emotions threatens to overwhelm me, and I steady myself against the door.

Greg stands. 'I'm sorry, there has obviously been a mix up. I should go. Thanks for inviting me, champ, but maybe we should do it another time.'

I'm stuck, frozen in place. Now that the fear has drained away, I'm embarrassed about the kiss, bewildered at Joe asking Greg over, and wary as to why Greg had come— especially at this early hour.

'Um,' Greg says, gesturing to the doorway I'm filling. 'I can't…um…'

I follow his hand and realise I'm standing here in my Hogwarts t-shirt and sleep shorts, my Christmas present from Joe, slippers, and a serious case of bedhead. Every part of me burns with embarrassment.

I close my eyes, trying to blot everything out. I open them. No, this is as horrific as I imagined.

Greg brushes past me as I catch sight of Joe, his face about to crumple. 'Mum, please can he stay?'

I take a deep breath. I can do this. It's only one morning with my nemesis. 'It's okay, you can stay for breakfast.'

Greg turns, his hand reaching for the door handle. He catches my eye and raises an eyebrow. I nod, telling him it really is okay.

'Can I help with anything?' Greg asks as he walks towards me.

The face Joe turns to me is beseeching—don't take him away it begs.

'No, stay and watch TV, I've got this.' I walk away before I can see either of their relieved faces.

In the sanctuary of my kitchen I calm myself by pulling my messy hair into a ponytail before pulling out everything I need for pancakes. Focusing on the task helps me to banish memories of yesterday's kiss, and the queerness of Greg in my home watching TV with my son.

I put on some coffee and breathe in the smell. Seconds later a voice startles me.

'Could I trouble you for some of that coffee? I'm not used to being up this early,' Greg's hanging in the doorway as if he's not allowed to come in.

'It'll be a couple of minutes. I'll bring you some,' I say, not taking my eyes from the pancakes.

'I'm sorry about this. When Joe asked me yesterday I told him to check with you. I even gave him my number so you could text me if it wasn't okay.'

I sigh, my peace broken. 'It's fine. Really. He fell asleep in the car on the way home and I suspect it slipped his mind.' I flip the pancakes, then pour a couple of mugs of coffee.

'Milk's in the fridge, sugar's on the bench,' I tell him, passing him a cup.

'Thanks, black'll do fine.' He flashes a smile before retreating to the living room.

I finish the pancakes and ferry them into the lounge. While we eat, Greg and Joe keep up a constant patter about which Transformer is the best. While I'm used to this debate, I'm surprised Greg's so knowledgeable.

As if reading my thoughts, Greg catches my eye and chuckles. 'I have a niece and two nephews, so I try to keep up on all the trends.'

I take the empty plates out to the kitchen and make more coffee. Returning to the living room I pause for a moment. The domestic scene is everything I wished for Joe before he was born, but it was Carl, not Greg who I had dreamed into that picture.

Ignorant of my thoughts, Greg sits on the floor with Joe, letting him help transform the Optimus Prime action figure. My heart heavy, I hand him a new coffee and return to my seat.

As the two of them play, a part of me wonders what Greg's game is? Yesterday's kiss and turning up today—surely he can't be using Joe to get close to me?

'So, Greg, do you often have breakfast dates with strange kids?' I ask, watching him over the rim of my mug.

He chuckles. 'You've caught me out. I do have an ulterior motive coming today.'

'What's an alter motive?' Joe asks.

'Well, it's a bit like cheating,' Greg explains. 'Like I wanted to come here today to check you were okay, and to have pancakes. But I also wanted to ask your mum something.'

'Oh,' Joe say. 'I thought it might be something bad.'

I barely hear my son's words my heart is pounding so loud in my ears. 'You wanted to ask *me* something?' I say, trying to keep my voice even.

'Yes. I wanted to know if you sell your paintings? I'm doing a restoration, and Cathy is doing the interior design. We both thought the dining room needed something. I remembered your work from school and… well, I think one of your pieces would be perfect.'

Of all the things he could have said, I would never in a million years have expected this. My brows are drawing into a frown and I try to force them apart. If I'm honest, part of me was a little disappointed he hadn't asked me out—not that I would have said yes. The other part drifted up to the attic, where my canvas and paints had sat virtually untouched since the night I gave birth to Joe.

With Carl not around, I couldn't afford the luxury of being an aspiring artist. When Joe was a baby I got my teaching qualifications through night school, and now I teach art at my old high school.

'Mum doesn't paint,' Joe says before I could pull my thoughts into a coherent answer.

'You don't?' Greg asks 'I thought you went to art college—'

'I did, then, well, other priorities took over.'

Greg looks at Joe then back at me. I hold my breath, hoping he won't say anything about giving up my dreams for my son. I never want Joe to feel guilty, and I would make the same decision again in a heartbeat.

Greg turns back to Joe and says, 'When we were kids your mum used to paint, and she was pretty good at it.'

Joe half-turns towards me. 'Cool. Would you be able to paint some Transformers for my room.'

'Perhaps,' I demure, wishing this painful moment would end.

'And when she's finished, maybe you can persuade her to do something for me,' Greg says.

It's all I can do to keep myself from breaking into a stupid grin. Greg, the internationally renowned architect and my most critical schoolmate actually likes my art. Who knew?

Something buzzes. Greg pulls a phone from his back pocket. 'Oh, no. That can't be the time. Mum'll kill me if I'm late for lunch.'

He smiles ruefully, 'Thank you so much for breakfast, Abbie. And thank you for inviting me, Joe. I'll have to return the favour sometime.'

We see him out, and when he leaves Joe and I return to the living room. Somehow it seems empty without Greg there.

Back to Reality

'I've gotta go,' I say.

Cathy's laugh fills my earbuds. 'You can't drop a bombshell like that then go.'

'That's the thing about phone conversations—I so can. Besides, I see your fingerprints all over this. You must have put the idea in his head. I mean, you've been on at me often enough to get painting.'

The phone is silent. 'Cathy?'

'Yeah, sorry, dropped my phone. It was all Greg. He suggested one of your paintings would lift the dining room. I agreed, but before I could tell him you weren't painting, the owner joined us and the subject was dropped. I was surprised he even remembered you painted.'

That makes two of us.

'So?'

I frown. 'So what?'

'Are you going to do it?'

It took me a moment to work out what she was getting at. 'No! I don't have the time.'

'Mmm, I am sure you could find time if you wanted to. Gotta go. Talk later.'

I have dead air and kids are filing in for first period. I put my phone in the drawer.

As the week wore on and real life took over I forgot about painting, but not the kiss, or the physical attraction it awakened.

On Friday Joe was spending the night with Carl's parents and they were dropping him off at football in the morning. Child-free, I was able to join the rest of the teaching staff for end of week drinks.

I enjoyed the opportunity to let my hair down with friends. I even allowed myself to be talked into performing a couple of karaoke songs with them. In the history of karaoke performances, Eye of the Tiger and I Will Survive have never been so thoroughly butchered— but we had fun.

As we sat down I caught sight of a familiar figure. Greg was sitting in a booth, his back to our table, facing the stage. He half turned to go to the bar and my stomach lurched. Greg caught my eye, and his smirk reminded me of all those cutting comments from our school days.

I picked up my drink as if I hadn't seen him, hoping he wouldn't come over and mention our not so noteworthy performance. I was surprised to find a little part of me was disappointed when he didn't appear at our table. Curiosity nagged, and I took a quick peek. Greg's back was to me, but the sleek, dark haired woman sitting opposite him was more than visible.

If my heart had been thawing a little towards Greg after the kiss last weekend and his visit on the Sunday, it froze completely as I studied his new girlfriend. She was exactly the type Mark described when he talked about his brother's conquests.

OMG, I can't believe I thought he was actually interested in me. I can't compete with that! That will teach me to believe people change.

I sipped some wine and turn back to my work mates, trying to recapture my earlier feeling of lightness.

The barman calls last orders and we decide to leave. As the cold air hits me, I stumble and grab for the door. *Really, when had I become such a lightweight. Two glasses of wine and I'm almost legless.*

'Here, let me help you,' a familiar voice says, and I want to crumple to the ground in shame.

'I'm fine,' I say, without turning.

'I know. But I also know alcohol and shoes that high don't always mix,' Greg tells me as his supporting hand on my back steadies me.

'It's okay, we've got her.' I was rescued by a gaggle of teachers who swept me away from my embarrassment. 'Come on Abs, we're on for some clubbing.'

By the time I convinced them I wanted to go home, not to a club, my head had cleared. In the safety of my kitchen I drink a glass of water before taking another upstairs. It was only 11:00pm and I was ready to crawl into bed.

Greg has a new girlfriend: I text Cathy.

He hasn't.

He so has: *Glossy black hair, fashion mag clothes.*

:-) *Jokes on you. New client.*

My fingers are poised. Hold on, a new client? Why am I so relieved?

Cathy pings, *What do you care?*

I don't!: I exclaim my indignation.

My phone goes quiet. I lie on the bed staring at the ceiling. *I don't care,* I tell myself. Yet in my head I replay Greg leaning in to kiss me, and his laughing face as he catches my eye over top of Joe's head. Finally I admit to myself what Cathy already guessed.

I roll over and pick up my phone: *Don't say anything to Mark.*

❄

The air was crisp and I snuggled into my jumper, stomping my feet to keep warm. The game was about to start, and there was no sign of Joe and his grandparents.

Finally their car swept down the street before screeching to a stop. The back door swings open. Joe emerges, heading for the field, leaving the door wide open.

I pop my head inside, reaching for Joe's overnight bag.

'Just like Carl,' Bess says, 'in too much of a rush to say goodbye.'

There was an undertone suggesting a lack of manners, which would be my fault. 'I'll get him to call you tonight. Or you could come and watch his game,' I say, already knowing that won't happen.

The car is silent. They had wanted to take Joe to their family lunch, but he had chosen to play soccer rather than spend the day with his much older female cousins. 'Okay, have a good time with Peter and the kids.' I shut the door and walk away, not prepared to get into another row.

After stowing Joe's bag in the car, I join Cathy on the sidelines. She is in full mum-swing. 'Grace, honey, this is football not dance.'

Grace stops mid-pirouette and stares blankly at her mother. Three months older than Joe, Grace's a pretty handy footballer, when she focuses on the game. Then again, all of the team have their moments. And now it's Joe's turn. The ball sails past as he stands talking to his opponent.

'Joe,' the coach shouts, 'you can make friends after. For now could you chase down a ball or two?'

'What's he like?' Cathy said. 'He'll have made friends with the entire team by the time we've finished.'

I nod my agreement. Joe doesn't have a competitive bone in his body, but he loves meeting new people.

'I don't know, it seems like a good defensive tactic to me.' My stomach lurches. 'I mean, that kid he's talking to is their best player, and he's not even interested in the game.' Greg chuckles.

I glance at Cathy with a meaningful, *why didn't you say he'd be here*, look. She ignores me, pretending interest in the game.

'Besides,' Greg adds, 'when I was his age I was more like Grace, dancing rather than playing my way through matches.'

'Go on,' Cathy says. 'You were star of our high school team?'

'I know.' Greg chuckles. 'Who'd have believed.'

The game ends in a 3 all draw, which may or may not have been contrived by the ref. The players shake hands and we're bombarded by hyper kids.

'Mum, can we have pizza?' Grace asks.

'Yeah mum, can we?' Joe joins in.

I catch Cathy's eye . She nods.

'Okay,' I say, and Grace rushes off to the cars before we can change our minds.

Joe looks up at Greg. 'Are you coming too?'

'Greg might have—'

'I would love to,' Greg says. 'It's not often I get invited to pizza parties.'

A Late Night Visit

Joe flaked early. A late night, followed by football, and a pizza lunch had been too much for him. The house felt quiet without his usual chatter.

I poured myself a glass of red wine and flicked through the channels. Nothing on. Perhaps an early night with a book I think, taking my wine upstairs. As I wander along the hallway to my bedroom I pass the loft door. It has been so long since I've gone up there.

Without a clear intention, I find myself opening the door and switching on the light. The next moment I'm standing at the top of the stairs staring at my old workspace.

A couple of half-completed paintings lean against the wall. I grimace. In truth I'd stopped painting a little while before Joe was born. I was in such turmoil my anger came through in the harsh lines and dark colours, turning my visions ugly.

I wandered over to the desk where my sketch pads and water colours were. Placing the glass on the table I flicked through sketches I hadn't looked at for over seven years. My heart quickened. I picked up a pencil and turned to a clean page.

As my hand flew, Joe's face started to appear. Soon he is fully formed, a Bumblebee Transformer in his hand.

I put the pencil down and stretch, the start of a smile forming on my lips. I turn the chair around searching for a suitable canvas, the picture already colouring itself in my mind.

A buzz interrupts my thoughts, and it takes a moment for me to process it's the doorbell. I check my watch. 10:05. Who would be calling now?

The buzzer rings again, prompting me into action least it wake Joe. I rush down the stairs and peer through the spy hole. Greg? What's he doing here? The doorbell buzzes again, followed by a knock.

'Alright,' I say, fumbling the locks. 'Keep your hair on.'

I haul the door open, and glare at Greg. Before I can speak he grins. 'Aren't you going to invite me in?'

I don't move. No, I'm not. Having him near me messes with my head, and I want to get back to my vision in the attic. Still, my heart says, he looks mighty fine the way those jeans hug his hips, and the way that t-shirt stretches across his chest, and are his eyes smouldering?

'Abbie?'

'Ah, no, it's late and I'm busy.' The words tumble out in a rush.

He raises an eyebrow. 'Busy? At ten o'clock?'

His smile irks me. 'I might have company.'

His expression says, really? 'The lights are off everywhere except the attic. And unless you have something kinky up there…'

His voice is deep and suggestive, and I feel a flush rise as thoughts of 50 Shades run through my mind.

'I, uh…what are you doing out and about?' Okay, it's not a great comeback, but I'm surprised I'm even able to string this together.

'I was driving around and I saw the lights on.' He stops speaking and I risk a quick glance, surprised to find uncertainty written on his face. 'I thought, it was… I wanted to. Oh. Dammit.'

My head rises in surprise at the anguish in his tone, just in time to meet his lips as he dips down to kiss me. It takes a moment for my head to catch up with my body. When it does I find my fingers tangled in his hair, drawing him to me as his hands on my back pull my body against his.

Oh man, I haven't felt like this since… no I've never felt like this. Fire rages through my body, and my one thought is "more, give me more". *Hold on!* My mind takes control again. *What the hell!*

I pull away and take a step back.

'Greg. What's happening here?' I ask, resisting the urge to fall back into his arms.

Surprise and hurt cross his face before it settles into a grin. 'I was trying to seduce you, but you never did fall for my charms. I'd hoped… now we're older… Are you still in love with Carl? I can't compete with a dead man.'

I shake my head, hoping to dislodge the feeling I'm in a sitcom living the twist where my childhood nemesis confesses he's attracted to me. No. I'm still here on the doorstep, with Greg looking like he wants to devour me. Suddenly my legs feel weak and my head is spinning.

'Abbie, are you okay?'

Greg helps me into the living room and settles me on the sofa, before heading into the kitchen. He returns a minute later with two glasses of wine. I take one, gulping down a mouthful, before putting it down. I need a clear head.

Greg places his glass on the table and waits. Finally, when my hands stop shaking, I say, 'Greg, explain to me what's going on here.'

He sighs. 'I had this plan. Get to know you, make sure Joe was okay with my being around… but I can see we have an "all cards on the table" situation here.'

'Damn straight, I'm tired of these head games. For years all you did was criticise me, and now you turn up out of nowhere and we have this.' I wave my hand around. 'Whatever it is. I don't get it.'

Greg takes a deep breath, picks up his wine and downs half, then stares into the glass.

'Here goes. When I was a gangly teenager my brother brought home his girlfriend and her friend. I didn't think much about her until I saw her art. Her pictures were amazing, and creative, and when I saw them I thought I could see into her soul.'

I can't believe what I'm hearing. I want to argue, to object, but I can see Greg is struggling with this. He takes another mouthful of wine.

'By then, she's dating someone else. He was a jerk but she couldn't see it. I tried to tell her, but words have never been my thing.'

As stares into his wine, I try to imagine teenage Greg actually liking me enough to bother warning me off Carl. Through a different lens, I could see that might have been his motivation.

'Then I went to university, and travelled round the world. You'd think I would have forgotten her, but then she turns up at my brother's place and I'm the same tongue-tied teenager I once was. Only, this time I can't just leave. I want a life here, and I want her in it.'

I can't believe it. Greg, the boy… the man who was so self-assured, who I believed wanted to change me, is saying he wants me—saying the attraction I've been feeling isn't one sided.

'So, now you know,' he finishes.

I reach over and take his glass, putting it on the table, before leaning towards him and whispering, 'Now, why didn't you say that in the first place.'

I close the gap between us and capture his lips with mine.

Acknowledgments

A book takes a community to write, and I want to thank the lovely Nicole and my friend Ros for Beta reading all these First Kiss Stories. Without a doubt these stories would not be what they are without them.

And thank you to AmandaJane from QuillandInk for the final polish. You can find her on fiverr.com.

And, as always, love and thanks to Jim and Sam for supporting my mad, crazy writing addiction, and to my dog trouble who is always with me when I'm writing.

About the Author

Lee Williamson started writing and publishing as a fantasy author under the pen name Vivienne Lee Fraser. She then decided to try writing in some of her own favourite genres.

The First Kiss Series is her dipping her toe in the water. She will fully emerge herself with some full length Cosy Mysteries later in 2023/24, and has a full scale romance story brewing as well.

In the meantime, her First Kiss stories will be realising monthly at least until the end of 2023. Follow her to keep up with all the new stories.

facebook.com/leewilliamson66

Instagram.com/leewilliamson66

tiktok.com/@leewilliamson66